Dream Keeper

SAVANNAH WILDE

! Content Warning !

This book contains high levels of spice. We're talking fiery-hot, touch-me-and-I'll-burst-into-flames kind of spice. Inside, you'll find:

🔥 Group activities (some might call them orgies, we call them "team bonding")
🔥 Female on female, male on male, and every delicious configuration in between
🔥 Wolf shapeshifters who *do* know how to use their teeth (and tails)
🔥 The Sandman finding love—and no, he's not just putting people to sleep anymore
🔥 Magic, moaning, mating bonds, and mythical beings getting freaky

If you blush easily, read with a fan. Or a cold drink. Or both.

If you're under 18, close this book and go read about unicorns or taxes.

For everyone else—welcome to the wild side. You've been warned. 😈

For any mortal who dares to dream...

Chapter One

SANDMAN

MY WORLD WAS CRUMBLING.

Earthquakes shook my diminishing land, echoing the pain in my chest. One after another, causing the ground to tremble and plaster to fall from the palace walls. Balustrades toppled from the balconies into the raging ocean, creating fatal drops. I didn't dare leave the palace, and guarded Marguerite every second of the day.

Staircases ended in piles of rubble, cutting off our access to several of the rooms and destroyed gardens. No longer could Marguerite and I take an evening stroll through the landscaped lawns and discuss the wonder of human dreams. It had been weeks since we'd managed an uninterrupted dinner, and there were only the two of us here. In all the years I had stood sentry over Dreamland, I'd never seen it fallen into such disrepair.

She had been my assistant for decades. Her in the library, me in the sand cellar. Dinner at seven to discuss our day's work. Together we ensured the dreams of mortals were kept safe, that nightmares were held at bay, that humans didn't bring their reveries into reality.

During the last week, I had left my duties several times per day to ensure Marguerite was not buried by books and files in the underground library. I couldn't bear the idea of breaking in another assistant.

Struggling against the alarming shudders, I strode into the palace meeting hall to find Marguerite cowering behind a marble pillar. *The Cat* was glued to her legs, its plaintive mews barely audible over the crashes of falling stone. Chunks of plaster fell from the ceiling as the earth shook again. I ran to Marguerite, cradled her in my arms, and protected her head against my chest.

"How long are these going to last?" she asked, daring to peek out from my protective hold.

"I don't know," I murmured. I held her until the earth stopped shaking, stroking her bright red hair, trying to soothe her. But I had no experience at it. My talents for empathy and protection had only extended thus far into the ability to deliver fantasies in mortals' dreams. Nothing real. Nothing concrete. Nothing like this.

Her fragile heart beat against my chest, revealing her fear. Mine remained steady and sure, as it always had been, as it always would be. Immortal. Endless. A gift bestowed by the gods.

When the last chunks of plaster had settled, and one entire marble column lay across the polished floor, Marguerite disentangled herself from my embrace and removed chucks of plaster from her hair.

"They're losing hope," she said, wiping dust from her iridescent cloak.

"Who are?" I asked.

"The dreamers." She took my hand and led me to the marble balustrade that overlooked my lands. One of the few that hadn't crumbled and fallen to the rocks below. I had been avoiding this particular view for over a week. She held my chin and made me look.

I gasped. My land was no longer the same. Gone were the infinite blue seas that stretched to the horizon, the tall ships sailing on their tempestuous waves. Gone was the city gilded in gold. Gone were the angels playing harps in the clouds, the absence of their sweet music leaving a hole in my chest. The grounds before me were barren and dying. Worse, a deep, dark nothingness surrounded everything. Encroaching. Engulfing. Swallowing my land.

"I tried to tell you," Marguerite said, her voice kind, no hint of the reproach I deserved.

She spoke the truth. During the last couple of decades, a foreign sadness had settled between my ribs. An emotion I hadn't experienced before and one I could only identify after a few years of research. Sad. How was I, the King of Dreams, sad?

My emotions weren't my own. They reflected the hope in the hearts of mortals. If Earth was dying, then dreams would too. And I would cease to exist. Then there would be only misery.

It had never happened before.

Marguerite turned to the library for answers. Dreamers dreamed every night, and those fantasies, or nightmares, became lines in the folders and books in the library. Ever expanding. Except for recently. Recently, the shelves had shrunk, the aisles had shortened, the files had thinned. But I had refused to believe my land would die. Refused to listen to Marguerite's warnings. After all, the old gods assigned me here. Surely nothing they decreed could ever go wrong.

Foolish. Of course I was. Everything they oversaw went wrong. I hadn't seen them for five centuries. I didn't know if they still existed.

"We need to do something," Marguerite said, a delicate hand gesturing to the rubble at our backs. "It won't be safe for us here much longer. If the dreamers stop completely...what will happen to us?"

The two of us lived in a marble palace. Everything shining white and gold. Beautiful arches and cozy niches. Bedrooms fit for any king, or god. But now, everything was decaying before my eyes. Dead vines wound between broken cobbles. A reeking stench filled the air. The well of nectar and the field of ambrosia had run dry months ago. Fires broke out everywhere, feeding uncontrollably on a destructive path through the forests, each one making a course for the palace.

"But what?" I asked, hating the note of panic in my voice. I had been alive for centuries, and I had never panicked. But my world had never tried to die before.

Marguerite squeezed my hand. "You need to get them dreaming again."

"But why did they stop?"

"There have been many trials. Natural disasters, pandemics, a dying planet...many of them are losing hope, refusing to believe in dreams, refusing to believe in a future."

"Where is Pandora?" I chuckled at my joke. Pandora had also been missing for centuries. She had brought pestilence to Earth, but she'd also brought Hope, and then conveniently disappeared.

"It's up to us, now."

"Us?"

"You."

"But how do I make dreamers have hope?" I asked.

"You must visit them personally. Show them their futures can be bright, help them find their desires."

"I can't remember the last time I visited Earth," I said, watching a burst of steam and ash erupt from a newly formed crater. Fire filled the sky, raising the temperature, its sparks eating fields of brown grass. The earth shook again, and Marguerite clutched my arm. I held her until the tremor abated, and both of us eyed the approaching flames. The fire fed hungrily, as if desperate to reach us in our moldering palace.

It was no longer safe here. No matter how scared I was for myself, for my lands, I couldn't let any harm befall Marguerite. She was the best assistant I'd had. I owed her a future.

"There's no time like the present."

"But where do I begin?" I asked.

"With Rose Turner." Marguerite plucked a file from the air. She was the only one capable of transferring the files from the library into my arms. A power not even I possessed.

"And who, pray tell, is Rose Turner?" I asked, as I thumbed through the pages.

"Late-thirties. A waitress. Lives in council housing

and uses all her money to pay for her grandmother's care. She's in a dementia home. The grandmother."

"I see."

"Rose has two pairs of shoes to her name and not much else," Marguerite continued. "Her boss is miserly and hasn't given her a raise for three years."

"And what is it Rose desires?"

Marguerite smiled. A smile that lit up the crumbling palace and reflected off the marble columns. A smile that touched the corners of my heart. A smile that gave me the confidence we were doing the right thing. A smile that filled me with hope. *Hope.*

"She loves books."

"Maybe I should give her your job?"

Marguerite frowned.

"I'm joking," I said. "You have served me well over the years. I could deal with no other."

"Thank you," she replied softly, tightening the belt of her cloak. "Back to Rose. She loves books. Romance books, specifically. *Erotic* romance books." She blushed. Adorably. In all our years together, I'd never seen Marguerite blush. "Shifter, erotic romance books, to be precise."

"And what, pray tell, is a shifter?"

"A person who can turn into an animal. The shifter romance genre centers on wolves."

"Wolves?"

Marguerite's blush deepened. I had the urge to play with her, but one look at the broken land flowing from my dented balustrade, and I changed my mind.

"What do you know of these wolf shifter romances?" I asked.

"Nothing much," Marguerite said. "Only that it is Rose's desire to have her own wolf."

"To have?" I asked.

"For him to ravage her." She coughed. "Sexually."

Chapter Two

SANDMAN

I ARRIVED on earth in the middle of a lightning storm. It was the only way I could travel and not raise suspicion. Moving between dimensions caused an energy shift, and the results were always...powerful. Often, I left glass sculptures behind, the product of my sand and lightning. Sometimes I would reclaim them and gift them to Marguerite. Other times, I would offer them to the gods.

I stood outside the roadside diner at midnight on a Tuesday, listening to the racket mortals called rock music, attempting not to stick my fingers in my ears. Cars streaked by on the highway at my back, a flash of lights and cacophonous sound. Muted stars peeked from behind gray storm clouds. A three-legged dog barked at the overflowing dumpster. The reeking stench seemed to follow me from Dreamland.

Two drunks stumbled out of the diner to the accompaniment of a discordant bell tied to the door. They threw their arms around each other and shuffled to a dented pickup truck, giggling like schoolgirls. They shouldn't be driving. How many dreams might they destroy with one stupid decision?

Using a pinch of sand, I blew a small gust toward them. The sand flew on the wind, plucking the car keys from the hand of one and sending it down a storm drain. They'd spend the next half hour looking for them, and then perhaps fall asleep on the wet pavement.

I walked into the diner, the bell clanging discordantly, to find a restaurant full of late-night patrons. Truckers eating pie after a long stretch on the road, a group of scantily clad college students giggling over a plate of French fries, a couple of people in booths on their own, drowning their spirits in coffee or liquor. I ignored them all and walked into the staff area without drawing attention. Walking with the shadows was a talent of mine.

I found Rose in a small staff room rolling an unlit cigarette over her fingers. Her dark hair was unraveling from a messy ponytail, her lipstick fading, her mascara smudged at the corners of her eyes.

"Care for a light?"

"I don't smoke," she replied without looking up.

I let out a soft chuckle. "But you used to."

She looked up, met my eyes. Hers were dull and uninspiring. Perhaps I could change that. "A long time ago."

I pulled up a stool opposite her in the cluttered room. Just a table and three stools, an overflowing ashtray, dents and scuff marks decorating the four yellowing walls. The smell of grease and onions hung in the air.

"You shouldn't be in here," she said, half-heartedly rising from her seat. "This room is for staff only."

"I'm not here to buy food or drink," I replied.

She stared at my face, a hint of fear running through her eyes. "What are you here for, then?"

I raised a palm to show her I meant no harm. "I'm merely here to help."

Easing herself back onto her stool, she laughed. "Help? Unless you've got about twenty grand lying around and the ability to pay my electric bill, I don't think there's much you can do."

Her laugh was fake. A practiced reaction to show people she was tough. But I sensed the loneliness in her kind heart, the longing to make a real human connection. To feel not so alone. If I didn't have Marguerite...

"Unfortunately, I can't magic money out of thin air, but I can give you hope."

The cigarette in her hands snapped in two. "I don't need hope. I need a new life."

"Perhaps I can give you that for one night."

She averted her eyes and smoothed down her skirt. But I didn't miss the color rising in her cheeks.

"Who are you?"

I countered with another question. "What is it you dream of, Rose Tanner?"

"Dreams? Dreams are for the young."

"You're not so old, Rose Tanner."

She fiddled with the butt of the broken cigarette. "It's kind of you to say so, but I'm too old to be flattered."

"And too young to give up on your dreams."

A sad smile formed on her lips as she brushed the flecks of tobacco into a trashcan. "What would you know about dreams?"

"They don't call me The Sandman for nothing."

She laughed, a beautiful sound that eased some of the anxiety surrounding my heart. "I feel like I can trust you. Like you can see straight into my soul."

I cupped her cheek with my hand. She leaned into my touch, her dark eyes whirring with flecks of hope.

"Tell me what you desire," I said.

Her eyes rolled back, and she fell limp against my hand. I eased her back onto the stool as sleep took her and found the images deep in her subconscious. So this is what a shifter was. The power. The masculinity. The passion. I could understand the attraction.

"You shall have what you desire," I told her. "At least in your dreams."

I left her on the stool, propped against the table, granting her the fulfillment she craved.

Chapter Three

ROSE TANNER

ROSE RAN through the midnight forest, tripping over unseen roots. Branches whipped her cheeks, stinging her flesh and drawing blood. The trees blotted out the moon and what little light she had to see by. The rich, loamy scent of wet soil surrounded her. It was all she could smell. It seemed that was all there was. The dirt and the trees. And him. No one to hear her scream. No one to call for help. She'd dropped her phone half a mile back and now fumbled about in the darkness.

She called her Grandma every Wednesday. That was tomorrow. How could she do that without a phone? She'd have to visit in person, take the afternoon off work. Money down the drain. She was already in debt over her eyeballs. Soon she'd have to move her grandmother to a state facility. One of the ones where they drugged them to keep them docile and didn't change their adult diapers for days.

Tears glistened in Rose's eyes as she ran. She would

never allow that. She'd kill them both before she allowed that to happen.

And so she ran. She ran from her fear. Ran from her burdens. Ran from the thing following her in the woods. Even though every cell in her body was screaming at her to stop and lie down. To just *stop*, she ran.

The farther she went, the faster she ran. Her breath came in labored gasps, but her worries fell by the wayside as she charged through the unforgiving forest. A sprinter's pose. Arms pumping, legs pumping, heart pumping. She saw only the path ahead. Heard only the thundering footsteps at her back, and her own galloping heart.

Her uniform was cut to shreds, her dark hair tangled with sticks and leaves. But she wasn't scared. Not entirely. There was an exhilaration to this chase.

It followed her, the unseen thing. Growling and tearing at the undergrowth. It was faster than her. She knew she couldn't outrun it. She knew it would catch her, eventually, and she welcomed the unavoidable conclusion.

Rose stopped to catch her breath, resting her hand on the rough bark of a towering oak. There were pine needles in her shoes and her laces were untied. She sucked pine-scented air into her spent lungs, willing more adrenaline to her limbs. A growl reverberated through the forest, sending a chill up her spine. She searched the darkness for the source, but it remained hidden, whatever it was.

When another growl ripped through the night, Rose ran. She stumbled over fallen trees, leaped over shrubs, never daring to glance over her shoulder. Sweat coated her skin, pooled in the small of her back, ran between her legs.

Rose tripped, flew through the air, landing badly on her ankle, and rolled down a shallow incline. She came to a stop against a tree trunk, muttering obscenities and cradling her ankle. The stench of moss and recent rainfall surrounded her. Owls hooted and unseen things rustled the undergrowth.

Still dressed in her waitress uniform, the skirt split and spoiled, Rose cursed the amount of money her boss would dock her for a new one. Gritting her teeth against the pain, she again wondered how she'd gotten here. The last thing she remembered was the mysterious man dressed in black who'd visited her at the diner during her only break. The dark hair with the shock of white running down the middle. The ice-blue eyes that penetrated her soul and seemed to understand her deepest desires. And now here.

The scratches and bruises she could bear, but the pain lancing through her foot and leg made her clench her jaw and hiss out a scream. This wasn't fun anymore.

The bushes rustled. Eyes glinted in the dark. It had found her. Whatever it was.

A white wolf emerged from the darkness. The largest animal she'd ever seen. It peered at her through the night, its beautiful fur aglow with impossible moonlight. Its midnight eyes fixed on her, and it chuffed. Then raised its snout to the sky and released a mournful howl.

Rose screamed. There was little else she could do. The wolf cut off its howl and regarded her solemnly.

They stared at each other. Fear and pain leached out of Rose's body. Something else took its place. Something she couldn't identify. Something she'd thought she'd lost a long time ago.

She watched the wolf shimmer and shake, its fur transforming to something else, its skeleton taking on a new shape. Within seconds, a man stood before her. Tall and virile. Muscular and deliciously sculpted. Naked and glorious.

The wolf man lifted a fur of some kind and wrapped it around her trembling shoulders. "I didn't mean to frighten you," he said in a rough voice. "But I simply can't let you get away until you have been fulfilled."

"Fulfilled?" she managed to ask.

"That is your deepest desire, is it not? To be fulfilled by a wolf?"

Rose cast her gaze around the dark forest. She couldn't make anything out in the trembling foliage, and turned her eyes back to the exquisitely naked male. She forgot to feel afraid as she examined him.

Tall and muscular, with sinewy forearms and sculpted thighs. A light downy hair covered his body, traveling across his chest, down his stomach, arriving at the dense clump surrounding his intimate parts. He didn't hide them, didn't try to shy away, only smiled as she took in his size.

Her heart rate picked up speed once more and a dull ache formed in the junction between her legs.

Thick hair tumbled to his shoulders in ragged waves and rugged facial hair leaned him a mountain look.

Someone who was used to surviving in the wild, running with the wolves.

"I don't know what my deepest desire is," she whispered, raising her eyes to meet his.

He smiled. A smile of warmth and welcome and the promise of fulfillment. "But it is one of them?"

"Oh, yes," she managed, biting down on her lip. "But why would you want me?"

The man frowned, the line on his forehead lending him a deeper handsomeness. "Why wouldn't I?"

Rose looked down at her frail hands, scarred from years of scalding water at the diner, the lack of a ring, the sunspots on her skin, the patch of insistent eczema on her palm. So scarred. So imperfect. She was the opposite of desirable.

The man crouched and cupped her cheek with one large, warm palm. "You are worthy, Rose Tanner. Don't doubt that."

The warmth spread from her cheek and down her neck, across her chest. It circled her breasts, swept the length of her stomach, and gathered in the soft, sensitive area between her legs. Every cell in her body tingled. Desire flamed, drowning her earlier self-doubt.

"What do you want from me?" she asked.

He smiled again. Such a delicious smile that charmed her to the core. "I only want to pleasure you. Will you at least allow me that?"

She nodded, smiled coyly, and gave her inhibitions to the night. "I should at least know your name."

"Aiden," he replied simply, then drew her face close to

his. His lips brushed her cheek, swept down the length of her neck, and paused at her throat.

Aiden took the animal skin from her shoulders and laid it on the ground. He plucked her from the earth in his powerful arms and placed her across the furs. "Tonight is all for you," he whispered in her ear.

She lay back on the luxurious white fur, knowing this moment wasn't real, knowing the man who'd visited her in the diner had somehow granted her a wish. She gave herself to it. Regrets were useless here. This night she planned to embrace, and then treasure on the subsequent lonely evenings. Tonight, she would live out her fantasies.

Aiden brought his lips back to hers, sweeping his tongue inside her mouth, teasing her until she responded with equal force. One of his hands cupped the back of her head, the other drifted to her waist, drawing circles through the thin fabric of her ruined uniform. A longing burned inside her, stirring between her legs. A sensation she'd ignored for years and almost forgotten until now. But she wouldn't deny herself any longer.

"What is your wish, my love?" Aiden growled in her ear.

"For this night to never end," she gasped as his hand trailed below her navel.

"Then you shall have that wish," he replied, his soulful eyes staring down at her. "At least for tonight."

He kissed her again. The warmth of his lips traveled along the line of her jaw, to the hollow of her throat, down between her breasts. She arched her back to meet his delicious kisses, wanting more. Needing it more than air.

"Not so fast," he said, trailing a hand down her cleavage. Unhurried, he unbuttoned her dress. Painstakingly slowly, one button fell loose at a time until he reached the tip of her panties. His hand rested on her warm skin, circling her navel, threatening to descend lower.

"Please," she muttered against his neck. "I want you."

"And I want you."

His hardness pressed against her thigh. Mustering some courage, she reached for him and circled her hand around his pulsating girth. He groaned, an animal noise, filling her ears.

She smiled. "Who's the prey now?"

He laughed, a sensual sound that traveled over the rustling leaves. A cool breeze swept across her bare shoulders, tickled the exposed skin of her stomach.

Aiden rolled the dress from Rose's shoulders, helping her arms out of the sleeves, pushing it down until the garment gathered at her waist. Rose pushed it lower, past her knees, until she was able to kick it off. Now she wore only a bra and panties.

"How beautiful you are," Aiden said, his hair falling across her face, his lips torturing the skin between her breasts.

Pulling her bra away, he cupped a hand over her breast, circled his thumb around her nipple, gently teasing until she grew erect. He replaced his hands with his mouth, his tongue circling, his teeth gently nipping. The warmth of him leached into her.

A hot wetness spread between her legs, making her

arch her back and press her hips against him. She reached for him once more, her hand circling his hardness, stroking softly, then more insistently.

"What are you doing to me?" he said. "I'm supposed to be pleasuring you."

"It works both ways," she replied.

He bit her ear, eliciting a shriek of pleasure. She dug her teeth into his shoulder until he raised his head and laughed at the dancing moon.

He shifted himself on top of her. His nakedness sent her wild. Maybe it was the moon. Maybe it was The Sandman. Maybe it was finally allowing hope into her heart.

She clutched his buttocks, pulling him tight against her. He lowered his mouth to her breasts and tore her bra way. Then ripped her sheer panties from her legs. It didn't hurt. His wolfishness. She wanted it all.

She pressed herself against him. Both of them naked. She gripped him tightly, clutching him harder, digging her nails into his flesh.

"I want you. Now. I need this. I need you. *Please*," she begged.

"We have all night," Aiden replied with a wolfish grin.

He kissed her lips, then her throat, then each breast. His mouth trailed lower, circled her navel, then his tongue ran across the sensitive part of her stomach. He paused to look at her, his eyes glinting in the moonlight, promising fulfilment of all her wishes.

"Please," she whispered.

His warm tongue drifted into the soft downy curls between her legs. She groaned as the longing built. The tingling that could only be satisfied in one way. The muscles in her center spasmed, begging for his entrance.

Aiden pulled on her short curls with his lips, igniting an intense desire, then his tongue brushed the point of her need, making her gasp more than once.

"Aiden!" she cried into the night.

"I am here, my Rose," he replied with a growl, and bit into the flesh between her legs.

His tongue raked over her skin, danced between her folds, eliciting yelps of desperation. She arched against him, laced her hands behind his head, pushing him deeper. He thrust his tongue deep, drawing out an agonizing bliss that she could only control by clenching her jaw.

"Aiden!" she cried again.

Her vision swam as the pleasure between her legs overtook her limbs. The ecstasy built in a wave she couldn't contain, swarming through her veins, hammering through her silken depths until her body shuddered uncontrollably.

"Aiden!" she screamed with all her might, uninhibited, finally allowing herself to feel it all. The wave of pleasure almost crushed her. Everything tingled and spasmed, and she writhed against him, wanting more.

"I'm here, my darling Rose," he said, his lips now at her ear.

She kissed him, gasped against his neck. "I never knew it could feel that way."

"I'm not done with you yet."

"It's too much," she replied.

Aiden chuckled and kissed her roughly, muting

further protests. He took her hand and pressed it close to his hardness. She circled her fingers around his girth and began with gentle strokes. Aiden groaned in her ear, bit down on her skin, dug his fingers into her arms.

She quickened her pace until his groans filled the forest, then he grabbed her wrist and made her stop. "This is not how it's done."

"How is it done?"

He kneeled, placed his hands under her buttocks, and shifted her closer. He lifted her hips and pressed the tip of his rigid shaft into her opening.

"Yes," she murmured.

He smiled down at her, his eyes alight with mischief.

"Please, Aiden."

"Like this?" He pushed into her, but only an inch.

"You're teasing me," Rose protested.

"Indeed."

"I want you."

Aiden thrust into her, half of his length disappearing into her welcoming warmth. She contracted against him, trying to gather his hardness deeper, but he resisted her encouragement.

"*Please*, Aiden."

She lifted her hips to take more of him, digging her nails into his buttocks, pulling him hard against her.

Aiden let out a groan and collapsed against her, his throbbing penis entering her fully, filling her depths.

"Deeper," she commanded.

Aiden pressed deeper. He thrust into her with quickening strokes.

"Harder," Rose said.

Aiden's next thrust powered through her, taking her to a new brink. Her muscles spasmed around him, warning her she was close.

"Faster," she said.

Aiden quickened his pace, pushing into her with a force she didn't know she could take. He thrust again and again, raising his face to the moon, howling with the other wolves in the forest. He kept her on the edge, slowing when he sensed she was near, sometimes pulling out completely when she shuddered against him.

"Please, Aiden," she begged. Never had anyone drawn out the experience quite like this. It was exquisite. Painful. And she couldn't stand it a moment longer.

"Aiden!" she screamed.

He plunged into her, filling her, sending the spasms pulsing through her body. She contracted against him, drawing him deeper as her scream woke the night. She clutched him to her, bit into his shoulder, pulled at his hair, gripped his buttocks.

The orgasm thundered through her. Her warmth surrounded his pulsing hardness, and she urged him deeper still. Orgasm after orgasm washed over her. She arched her back, flexed her limbs, held onto him with all her strength, prolonging the sensations that filled her from her head to her toes, and everywhere in between.

"My darling, Rose," Aiden growled as his wetness burst from him, filling her, eliciting another wave of pleasure.

When it was done, he collapsed against her, and she held him in her arms.

"Thank you, Aiden," she said.

"No, Rose. Thank *you*." He rolled off her and cradled her close. "I hope that was everything you desired."

"And so much more," she said, as she watched the stars through the trees.

Aiden kissed her. "We still have the rest of the night."

Chapter Four

SANDMAN

I STOOD with Marguerite at the balustrade overlooking my realm. The fire was gone, the brown grass no longer charred, steam no longer erupting from explosive vents. But the black nothingness hovered at the edges of the land, threatening.

"It wasn't enough," I said, unable to cast my gaze upon my broken home for another second. Something in my chest lurched. I couldn't even meet Marguerite's eyes. We'd been ruling over mortals' dreams for so long, and it had fallen apart on my watch. I was a disgrace. Not fit to fulfill the role of Sandman any longer. I didn't fear the absent gods who might return and strip the title from me, but I couldn't bear to meet the judgement in her eyes.

"Sandy," she said, using my nickname, the one only she was permitted to use. But her use of it or her gentle tone couldn't lift my spirits.

She took my chin in her hand, her touch delicate and warm, and made me look at her.

"Sandy," she said again. Although our surrounding

landscape was a mess, Marguerite remained radiant. Her red hair burned with a fierce intensity and her pale skin glowed with a saintly aura. She'd never looked so exquisite. She pressed her fingers into my chin and smiled at me. "One dreamer can't save your land. It will take all mortals to rebuild Dreamland."

Fear prickled at the nape of my neck, the hollow of my throat, and slicked my palms. "I can't possibly visit every dreamer. There isn't enough time before my lands are decimated. It's hopeless."

I ripped my chin out of her soft grasp, pressed my hands into the cold balustrade. I kept my gaze down, not daring another look at the destruction beyond.

"Nothing is hopeless." Marguerite placed a hand over mine. "You don't need to visit every dreamer. Just visit a few. When the desire spreads, the mortals will start dreaming again. And your palace will be restored."

Glancing over my shoulder, I noted the piles of marble rubble, the collapsed arches, the dented gold, the hole in the domed ceiling that gave way to a smoky gray sky. "I don't care about the palace. I never have."

"What do you care about, then?"

I frowned, looked upon her pleasing face as if the answer might be hidden there. "I was made to be the Keeper of Dreams."

"That is your job," Marguerite said. "But what of *your* dreams?"

I whipped my head around, scanning the shadows for eavesdroppers. What she said was close to blasphemy. If the gods were listening, they wouldn't be pleased.

"I am without desire," I replied, ignoring the heaviness in my chest.

"Ridiculous."

"Marguerite," I snapped. A spike of guilt pricked me when she flinched. It pained me to see the hurt in her eyes. "You must be careful what you speak of."

"Every living creature has a right to a dream," she said, defiance straightening her shoulders.

"I am not alive. Not really. Not in the way you're suggesting."

"But you could be."

"No. It is impossible."

We stared at the motionless land. The sun hung low in the red sky, giving the dry earth a blood-filled look. I had to reach more dreamers. I had to protect these lands to give mortals a safe place to live out their desires. If they lost hope...it didn't bear thinking about.

"What is it *you* desire?" I asked her.

"To be here with you," she replied instantly.

I laughed. "That is not a very high ambition."

"It is all I need."

"And this is all *I* need," I said, sweeping a hand at my lands.

She looked at me, her gaze stripping my lies away. But I couldn't admit to the truth. I had a place here. People to protect. I would never abandon my post. I would never give in to hope. "If you say so."

"I do." I averted my gaze so she would drop the conversation. "Who should I visit next?"

With a soft sigh, Marguerite plucked another file from the air and handed it to me. "Samantha Morrison."

I opened the file and read the information about the young woman. "She is happily married with three children? Wasn't that her dream?"

"When she was young," Marguerite replied. "But dreams change."

"And now what does she want?"

Marguerite placed both hands on the balcony, watched *The Cat* pick a path over the rubble below. "Sometimes desires are dangerous. Which is why it's best to fulfil them in our dreams."

"I agree. It prevents people hurting others."

"She is happily married, loves her husband and children dearly—"

"Would give her life for them, I see that from her file," I said. "But she desires something secret?"

"She does," Marguerite said, twiddling the fastening of her cloak. "When she was at university, she kissed her best friend. They were drunk, it was a onetime thing, they remained friends for many years. Until family life made them both busy and her friend moved abroad. But Samantha has always wondered about that kiss. The desire and attraction she felt. She is confused about her sexuality. That perhaps it's not just men she desires."

I raised my eyebrows. The sexual desires of mortals filled a large percentage of Dreamland, but I hadn't stopped to consider the emotions behind their fantasies. That wasn't part of my job description. I managed dreams and nightmares, keeping them apart, making sure there were no negative lasting effects on the waking world, protecting the minds of dreamers while they were here.

But recently I'd had more time on my hands. Time to think. To wonder. To *feel*.

I'd never pondered the physical sensations dreams evoked. Rose Tanner's experience had piqued my curiosity.

"What does it matter which sex she desires? Or if she desires both?"

Marguerite smiled at me like one does to a child. "It is more complicated on Earth. There are prejudices, and she's worried how her husband might react..."

"And so we must fulfil her desire in her dream, so she doesn't hurt those she loves in her waking life."

"Precisely."

I snapped the file closed. "That should be easy enough."

Chapter Five

SANDMAN

I ARRIVED in another lightning storm, the second in as many days, and landed on a narrow footpath lining the gardens of a row of quaint houses. The dwellings were small, but well maintained, and children played on a village green, their shouts of delight warming my soul. Children dreamed, constantly. None of them had given up hope. But there weren't enough of them to sustain my world. Not since anxiety had wormed its way into many of their hearts.

I found Samantha Morrison hastily snatching her laundry from a line, noted something secret behind her eyes. A hint of sadness that seemed to match the emotions taking over my soul. The recognition made me hesitate. Made me feel like an intruder. But I was here to do good things.

She cast furtive glances at the rolling gray clouds, muttering under her breath. I watched her from the garden gate, a small wooden barrier falling off its hinges and peeling with paint.

"Samantha Morrison?" I enquired, pushing the gate open. My long black coat swirled around my ankles in a sudden gust of wind. I was never hot nor cold, and I favored the anonymity the coat offered. There was little I could do about the brightness of my eyes or the swath of white in my dark hair.

She looked up, her mouth falling open, the laundry she'd been clutching now on the ground. "Who the hell are you? You can't just walk into someone's garden."

I gave her my most reassuring smile. It was small and understated, but the only one I was capable of. "Please do not be alarmed. I have only come to grant you your greatest desires."

She gaped at me, then threw her head back and laughed. So long and loud that a couple of birds took flight from neighboring trees.

"I think you've got your work cut out for you," she said once she'd composed herself, then gestured to the clothes she wore. The skinny jeans popular with so many mortals. A baggy plaid shirt, stained with baby food, her blonde hair wrapped up in a messy bun. "I'm far from desirable."

I approached and stood in the middle of her small garden. "I think you misheard. I'm not here to make you feel desirable...unless of course that is your dream. I'm here to grant you your wildest fantasies. For one night, anyway."

"I repeat, I think you've got your work cut out for you." There was no warmth in her face.

She was more guarded than Rose. Less willing to believe.

"You have nothing to fear from me," I said.

"Good," she replied. "Because my husband is inside."

A lie. I'd made sure she'd be alone.

"It's better to regret the thing you have done, then the things you have not," I said, hoping the melody of my voice would win her over.

"Bullshit," she said, grabbing her laundry from the ground and throwing it back in the basket unfolded.

Gray clouds scudded across the sky. The wind picked up and Samantha pulled her shirt tight across her chest. Rain sprinkled, dotting the garden, catching in my eyelashes.

I dared a step closer. She took a step back, the laundry basket clutched to her chest like a weapon.

"In your dreams, you can relive all your lost moments."

Her shoulders dropped, as if she'd decided she was no longer afraid. Perhaps my voice was finally working. "I don't have time for dreams. I don't even have time for a nap. Between homework and potty training, and Darrel's late nights, and turning down invitations from the girls, which I desperately need..." she cocked her head at me and narrowed her eyes. "And I don't know why I'm telling you all this."

"I'm happy to hear it," I said, blinking under the increasing rain.

Rain fell on her, soaking her shirt, dampening her hair. But she didn't react.

"Who are you?"

I splayed my hands. "I'm The Sandman. And I'm here to give you your most secret desires."

She pinched herself. "I really must be dreaming."

I winked. "Not quite yet."

Ignoring the rain, she leaned against the back of the house, obscuring half a leftover chalk drawing.

"An adult conversation. No stretch marks. A holiday in the sun. A night with my husband without interruption—"

"That's not it." I shook my head.

She raised an eyebrow. "You know my dreams?"

"Angelica." The name rolled off my lips. The name which represented all her regrets.

Color rose to her cheeks. "You don't know what you're talking about."

"Haven't you always wondered what could be?"

The color in Samantha's cheeks deepened. "How did you know that? I've never told a soul."

"It's my job to understand your fantasies."

"It's been so long...I'm married...I love my husband."

"But what if you could have both?" I asked. "In your dreams?"

She lowered herself into a plastic garden chair, the laundry basket wet and abandoned on the ground.

"Fuck me," she muttered.

"Then it shall be," I said as I removed a handful of sand from my pocket. I blew it gently in her direction and she fell asleep instantly.

Shielding her from the rain, I picked her up and carried her into the house. After laying her on a couch, I placed a blanket over her and watched her dream for a few moments. Before returning to my world, I retrieved the sodden laundry from the backyard and placed the items in the dryer, hoping I could save Samantha one small task.

Chapter Six

SAMANTHA MORRISON

Samantha startled awake, drenched through. Her hair was soaked, her clothes sodden, all the way to her underwear. She lay draped across the couch, under a blanket which had become damp from her wet clothes. She didn't remember lying down. The whirring sound of the dryer in the kitchen trickled into her consciousness, which reminded her of the long list of chores she had to get through before picking up the twins from school and the baby from nursery. She didn't have time for naps.

Making a mental list in her head, she swung her bare feet to the floor and felt the incapacitating throb of a dull headache knocking around the base of her skull. She didn't have time for headaches either. There was puree to make for the baby, and dinner to make for the twins, and the ballet lesson at 5pm, and then Darrel would be home and take over bath time. Perhaps then she could have a glass of wine...if the headache left her alone.

Samantha shook her head as tears heated behind her eyes. Would the list of chores never end? And still she sat in her wet clothes, uncaring about the dropping temperature or the coming cold that would surely settle into her lungs. And then who would take care of the kids?

The doorbell rang. She didn't have the energy to answer it. To turn away a religious zealot, or decline a rehabilitated convict selling cleaning products door to door, or refuse the nice neighbor from down the street who was always asking for sponsorship for her charity bike rides. Samantha didn't have the energy for any of it. So she sat on the couch and did nothing.

The doorbell rang again.

Samantha sighed and heaved herself out of the couch, raking her fingers through her unraveling bun. She trudged down the hall toward the front of the house. As she placed her hand on the doorknob, the bell rang for a third time.

Muttering a curse under her breath, she yanked the door open.

Her mouth fell open, and an involuntary gasp escaped her throat.

"Hey, you." Angelica smiled a beaming smile.

"A-A-Angel," Samantha stuttered.

She hadn't changed a bit in the ten years since they'd last seen each other. All luxurious dark skin and wild hair and the kindest and most thrilling smile.

"I'm back from Oz and you're the first person I wanted to see," Angelica said.

Samantha stood and gaped at her oldest friend. Absently, she touched a hand to her hair. Heat rose to her cheeks as she realized what a mess she was in her sodden jeans and oversized Mom shirt.

Angelica's smile slipped from her face. "Is this a bad time?"

Samantha could only shake her head.

Angelica looked past her and down the hall. "I love what you've done with the place."

They'd remodeled the house five years ago. They hadn't been able to afford much, but lightening the walls and new kitchen cabinets had given the house a more modern feel. But lately all Samantha saw were the dirty fingerprints smeared along the skirting and around light switches.

"Can I come in?" Angelica asked.

Samantha stared at her friend. The smart dark clothing, the high heels. She hadn't worn heels since the twins were born. Who was this person? Her oldest and closest friend, who now resembled a life she'd left behind long ago.

"Of course," Samantha said, holding the door open. "You've caught me in a rare moment alone."

"Good." Angelica smiled as she stepped into the house and kicked off her heels, tugging a large suitcase after her. "These shoes have been killing me. Remind me never to wear heels on a long-haul flight again."

"You came here from the airport?" Samantha asked as she led her friend to the kitchen and flicked the coffee machine into life.

"I did," Angelica replied, hovering in the doorway. "I'd love something stronger if you're up for it."

Samantha automatically checked her watch. 2pm. She couldn't remember the last time she'd drunk in the afternoon. But fuck it, why not? "I've got a nice Chablis I've been saving for a special occasion?"

"Sounds perfect." Angelica parked her suitcase near the table.

Samantha opened the fridge, took out the bottle of chilled wine. She removed glasses from the cabinet, the corkscrew from the drawer, her movements on autopilot. But her heartbeat betrayed her. It raced inside her chest, causing a flush to swarm over her skin. What was Angelica doing here? Not that it wasn't nice to see her friend again. After all, they'd kept in touch over the years on Facebook and the odd WhatsApp call. But now Samantha found herself tongue-tied as the memory from *that night* intruded.

She poured two glasses to the brim, sloshing some on the counter and almost emptying the bottle. Turning, she pushed one into Angelica's hand, keeping her gaze on her bare feet.

"I can't believe you came straight from the airport," Samantha said, risking a glance at her friend. The smell of vanilla and honeysuckle hung between them. Angelica's scent. One Samantha had almost forgotten about and now sent her stomach into freefall.

Angelica nibbled on her lower lip, then took a large gulp of wine. "I promised myself I would."

"Promised?" Samantha leaned closer. "Why?"

Angelica downed half her glass. "Because I left with regrets."

"What kind of regrets?" Samantha asked, her words barely above a whisper. She shivered, her damp clothes sticking to her skin.

Angelica closed the small distance between them and cupped Samantha's cheek, moved a lock of wet hair off her face. "You."

Samantha's cheeks burned, but she didn't dare step away, didn't dare ruin the moment.

"Is there any chance you might feel the same way?"

Samantha drained her own glass, then focused on Angelica. You were supposed to savor wine, but right now, Samantha needed a hit of courage. "Yes."

The smile that lit up her friend's face burned a fire in Samantha's soul and sent a dull ache pulsing between her legs. The memory of that night came back, stronger, more vivid. Alluring. Thrilling. Was it possible they could have more?

Angelica removed the glass from Samantha's hand. They stared at each other. Neither of them moved. Neither of them dared to breathe.

"What do we do now?" Samantha whispered.

Angelica moved forward, pressed her luxurious lips against her own. She hadn't been kissed by anyone but her husband for fifteen years. It was...strange, exquisite, perfect.

Angelica pulled back. "Was that okay?"

Samantha didn't reply verbally. She grabbed the V of Angelica's black silk shirt and yanked her closer. Samantha crushed her lips down on her friend's, drawing in her heat, pulling her lip into her mouth. Without thinking, she swept her tongue into Angelica's mouth, searching for her warmth.

Angelica's hands roamed Samantha's body, tugging at her shirt, sending buttons flying across the kitchen tiles.

Samantha didn't care. She could mend it later. Or throw it away. Whatever.

Samantha raked her fingers through Angelica's hair, pulling at her curls, loosening its bonds. Her hand swept down the length of Angelica's back, resting on her pert buttocks.

Angelica pulled Samantha's shirt off and cast it to the floor. Seconds later, the vest top followed. Samantha stood in the kitchen in bare feet, wet jeans, and a damp bra. But she'd never felt so warm.

Angelica's hands swept over her arms, caressing her skin, making goosebumps of desire rise. "I've wanted this for so long."

"Me too."

"I never stopped thinking about you."

Samantha tugged her friend toward the stairs, no longer afraid to look into her eyes. They held hands, but didn't make it farther than the foot of the stairs. Angelica took Samantha in her arms and kissed her once more. A slower kiss. Longer. Deeper. Taking her time to explore Samantha's mouth.

Samantha found the zip on Angelica's skirt, pulled it down, and tugged the material over her hips. Her friend remained in her shirt, panties, and stockings. The exquisite shape of her sent a fierce pang of need to the sensitive area between Samantha's legs. A desperate need ignited over her skin, centering as a deep ache within her damp opening.

"I haven't stopped thinking about you, like this, since that one kiss in college," Angelica breathed between kisses.

"You are in all of my dreams," Samantha said.

"Today belongs to us."

"No repercussions."

Gently, delicately, almost too slowly, Angelica unclasped Samantha's bra. The overstretched material hung from Samantha's arms, her breasts exposed. She was no longer ashamed. Her desire had taken over all her emotions.

They collapsed halfway up the stairs. Angelica was splayed on her back, her feet propped on one step, her knees spread.

Samantha took her in. The desire in her friend's eyes. The slight twitching of her hips. And the throbbing ache of her own need urging her own. She lowered her face for another kiss, used her tongue to trace a line across Angelica's jaw, down her throat, to the crevice between her perfect breasts.

Angelica cupped Samantha's breasts, gently at first, a thumb caressing one of her nipples. Her touch hardened, pinching and rubbing. Angelica took a nipple in her mouth, causing Samantha to let out a moan. Nothing existed apart from the two of them. She couldn't even feel the rough edge of the carpet under her knees.

As Angelica feasted on her nipples, Samantha's hands drifted to the junction between Angelica's legs. The sheer fabric of her friend's panties didn't hide her warmth or dampness. Samantha pressed the point of her need with her fingertips. Angelica groaned around her nipples.

With the wine now flowing through her bloodstream, giving her courage, Samantha reached for the elastic of Angelica's panties. She pulled them down over her thighs, past her knees, beyond her ankles, and chucked them over her shoulder.

Samantha looked at her friend. At the shaved area surrounding her glistening center. She licked her lips. The smell of Angelica's need thickened the air and drove pulses of desperation through the deepest part of Samantha's center.

Samantha lowered herself until her mouth was close to Angelica's clitoris. The smell intensified, driving her crazy. Without thinking, giving into the moment, Samantha lowered her lips to her friend's damp need. She took her clitoris into her mouth and sucked hard, kneading it with her tongue and teeth.

Angelica threw her head back and groaned. "Fuck me, I knew you'd be good at this."

Samantha didn't reply. She was getting high on the sweet taste of Angelica. Toying with her clit, probing it with her tongue, demolishing it with her lips.

"Oh. My. God," Angelica muttered, her hands digging into Samantha's hair.

Samantha pulled away. "I always wondered what you tasted like."

"Don't stop," Angelica murmured. "*Please* don't stop."

Samantha resumed devouring the sweet taste of her friend. She licked and kissed, nibbled and bit, making Angelica scream more than once. Samantha didn't stop. She pushed her tongue deep into Angelica's quivering center. Quickening her pace, she darted her tongue in and out, pushing harder, faster, until Angelica screamed once more. Samantha grabbed her friend's buttocks, pulling her closer, allowing her deeper access. As she kissed and nipped and licked and sucked, all she could smell was her friend. All she could taste was a sweet wetness. One she had craved for over a decade.

Angelica shuddered once more, then went slack against the stairs. "Oh, my God. You don't know what you just did to me."

Samantha straightened to her knees. "I think I have some idea."

Angelica stared at her, her dark eyes wild and wanting. "We're not done yet."

Samantha laughed. "We were on the way to the bedroom."

Angelica sat up and took her hand. "More wine?"

"We don't need wine anymore," Samantha replied.

They raced each other up the stairs, shedding clothing, letting it spill over the floor. Samantha's own need ached with a wild desperation.

Without stopping to admire each other's naked bodies, Samantha guided Angelica into the bedroom. Angelica pushed her down onto the bed and lay on top of her.

Their breasts fit snuggly against each other as Angelica lowered her head and devoured her with another kiss. She bit and sucked, bruising her lower lip, but Samantha didn't care. It brought back all the delicious memories of that night, so long ago, when they'd stopped long before they'd got this far. And now there was nothing to prevent them from fulfilling each other's desires.

Angelica pushed her hips against Samantha's. Her own desire pooled between her legs. She'd never been so turned on. All thoughts of her normal, boring, domesticated life had vanished from her head. She saw only Angelica. Felt only her own desire.

Angelica circled her narrow hips, pushing against Samantha's clitoris. Samantha gasped as spasms hammered through her, barely able to contain her need. Angelica was pushing her to the edge, and it wouldn't be long before she exploded.

Samantha arched her hips to meet Angelica's. Matching her rhythm, Samantha moved her hips too, their clitorises crashing against each other, making them both gasp. They'd long given up on kissing, could only be consumed by their own need for each other, by the pleasure, tingling at every crevice and swarming over their skin.

As Samantha reached her brink, Angelica inserted a finger deep inside her. She found her g-spot and stroked with quick movements. Unable to contain her pleasure, Samantha curled her toes, gripped the bed, almost shredding the sheets with her fingernails.

Another finger entered her, then a third. Angelica worked inside her, moving between her g-spot and her clit. Samantha's vision blurred. She snapped her eyes closed. Sweat slicked across her body, between their tightly pressed breasts.

"Let it go," Angelica whispered in her ear.

Samantha gave it all up. The sensation built between her legs, mounting unbearably until it had nowhere to go but to consume her shuddering body. The orgasm washed over her in a delicious wave. She cried out, not caring that the windows were open and the neighbors might hear. She released her desire, her pleasure, her dreams in that one undeniable scream. And still the orgasm stretched through her, pummeling her body, unwilling to be contained until every muscle shook with the intensity.

When it was over, Angelica's fingers remained inside her, and she sank into the mattress. Slowly, she opened her eyes, took in Angelica's radiant face. The glow of sex making her even more beautiful. Then she took in the figure standing in the doorway.

She bolted upright. "Oh, shit," she said, clasping the sheet to her chest. She didn't know why she was bothering; her husband had seen her naked countless times before.

"It's not what it looks like," Samantha said, heat rising to her already flushed cheeks.

With her fingers still inside her, Angelica grinned. "It's exactly what it looks like."

Darrel, dressed in black pants and a crisp white shirt, was removing his gold cufflinks from the sleeves. An amused smile played across his lips as he chucked the cufflinks on the bedside table. "Angelica called me on her way from the airport."

"She did?" It was the only question Samantha could manage as confusion whirled in her brain. "You're not mad?"

Darrel began undoing the buttons on his shirt. "She told me about your night in college. She told me about her desire to still have you."

Samantha noted the erection straining at the seam of

his pants. Her clit pulsed in response. This experience wasn't over yet.

"She did?" she repeated.

Darrel threw his shirt over the back of a chair. "I know things have been hard lately. With the kids, and no time for ourselves."

"They have," Samantha said, dropping the sheet to her lap, allowing the cool air to harden her nipples once more.

"So I arranged for my parents to have the kids for the night." Darrel stepped out of his trousers, letting them puddle on the floor. "So that we could both cheer you up."

"You're okay with this?" Samantha's head spun. Never in her wildest dreams had she thought Darrel would ever share her. Or she him. But this wasn't just any night. It was a dream. The best dream ever, one she felt fully, but just a dream. There were no regrets.

"I'd do anything for you," Darrel said, sitting down next to her on the bed.

Samantha took in the rugged stubble on his jaw, the desire in his bright blue eyes, the messed up hair after a day at the office. Her eyes trailed lower, down his throat, across his broad shoulders, down his sculpted chest. Lower still. To his hard abs, his muscular thighs, and then to his throbbing erection.

Darrel took Angelica's hand and removed her fingers from inside Samantha. He pushed them into his mouth and sucked off her juice.

A new flash of arousal ached between her legs. One that wasn't going away any time soon.

"Is this okay with you?" Angelica asked her as she stroked her breasts.

"God, yes," Samantha said, her breathing becoming shallow once more.

Darrel removed his tight boxer shorts, releasing an enormous erection that glistened with arousal. He sat back on the bed, and moved his fingers to her soft, downy curls.

Samantha groaned as Darrel kissed her and Angelica continued to caress her breasts. There were hands everywhere, two warm tongues licking and kissing her skin. She fell back onto the bed.

Darrel's longer fingers entered her, pushing against her need, pulling and stroking until a new orgasm built. She bit her lip to contain her pleasure, but couldn't prevent the anguished moans from escaping her throat.

Darrel removed his fingers just as she was about to come. "Not yet."

"Bastard," Samantha muttered.

With one strong arm, Darrel flipped her over, then yanked her hips up so she was kneeling on the bed with her elbows pressed into the mattress. Angelica shifted toward her head, moving her hips beneath Samantha's mouth. Samantha smelled her friend's sweet scent again and lowered her lips to her molten need.

Darrel pressed the head of his throbbing penis at her opening, and hovered there, teasing her. He reached around her waist and found her clit, kneading it between his fingers, making her cry out into Angelica's warmth, causing her friend to groan too.

Darrel eased into her, agonizingly slowly. He thrust

the length of his engorged shaft into her inch by inch, and then stopped. She adjusted around his girth, allowing her muscles to take him deeper, urging him to thrust.

She backed herself onto him, circled her hips against him, her butt pushing against his hips. He toyed with her clit, his fingers working faster, and finally began to thrust into her with even strokes. Each thrust was powerful and deep.

Samantha tightened herself around him, contracting her muscles, pulling him deeper. Her husband groaned as he pounded into her. He picked up the pace, penetrating her depths, filling her center, hammering spams of pleasure into her, his fingers working to drive her into oblivion.

She buried her face in Angelica's damp core, using her tongue to reach deeper with every one of Darrel's thrust. The three of them worked in tandem, all pleasuring each other at the same time.

Angelica flopped back on the bed, arching her hips, racking her fingers into Samantha's hair, and pulling her closer.

Darrel's thrusts became more urgent and insistent. The pleasure building deep inside Samantha could barely be contained. The pressure mounted, almost unbearable, the orgasm about to explode.

Darrel pounded into her, his length and girth filling every part of her, threatening to undo her. He let out a mighty roar as his seed squirted into her. At the same time, her own orgasm thundered through her body, stretching her apart, shuddering violent waves of bliss through every part of her. She didn't know how to contain it. And still it went on as Darrel continued to thrust and work his fingers on her clit.

She licked Angelica's dripping folds, sucked her clit into her mouth, moved her tongue deep inside. As Samantha cried out a second time, Angelica joined her, their moans reaching a new crescendo as they both spasmed and bucked against each other.

The orgasm stretched out, the most intense she'd ever experienced. Although centering deep inside her, it pulsed through her clit, and pushed out through her limbs, consuming her, making every cell in her body come alive with delicious sensation.

When it was over, they collapsed in a heap on the bed, limbs entwined, hands still caressing cooling skin, and promised each other there was more to come.

Samantha woke on the couch, her clothes still damp, but a smile on her face. She remembered every detail of the dream. Swinging her legs to the floor, she leaned back in the cushions and undid the buttons on her jeans. Although she had been more than satisfied in her dreams, her desire remained strong.

As she moved her fingers under the soft fabric of her panties, her phone rang. When she looked at the screen, Darrel's smiling face stared up at her. She answered it, her fingers moving lower, toward her silken lips. His deep, sexy voice came across the phone. It always got her off. She worked her fingers as she listened to him.

"I'm coming home early," he said.

"Uh-huh," Samantha muttered as the pleasure began to build.

"My parents are taking the kids."

"We can have a date," Samantha said, but she didn't really want to go out. She wanted him all to herself.

"And, uh, there's something else."

Samantha gasped as her fingers moved quicker. "Yes...?"

"I got a call from your old friend. Angelica?"

Samantha froze. "You did?"

"She has an interesting proposal."

Chapter Seven

SANDMAN

"THAT TOOK AN INTERESTING TURN," I said to Marguerite as we stood by the balustrade. Her hair was fastened in an elaborate style I'd never seen before, piled on top of her head, loose curls trailing down her neck. It suited her, allowed the weak sun to give color to her pale skin.

The Cat paced the marble balcony, stopping every once in a while to push its white head into my hand. I don't remember when it first arrived. One day it was simply there, stalking me from the shadows, hissing at me while I worked in the sand cellar. I'd never given it a name. We barely tolerated each other. More often than not it would hiss at me and scratch me, then retreat to the library to be with Marguerite. She had a way with animals.

Marguerite smiled. "Sometimes dreams really do come true."

I dared to cast a scrutinizing look at the view beyond the palace. The fires had ceased, the sky had turned a vague blue color, and clumps of green grass grew among the fields of brown. Birds flew through a clear sky, and I spotted a unicorn drinking from a shallow lake. "It's working."

"You got three for the price of one," Marguerite said.

"Three?"

"Samantha, Angelica, and Darrel all shared the same dream," she replied. "By granting one desire, you gave it to all three."

I smiled.

"But we aren't done yet," Marguerite said, pointing outside. Volcanoes continued to steam, cracks remained, splitting the land into pieces. Boulders tumbled from cliffs. and the waves went to war against each other in the steel gray oceans. Several marble pillars at our backs remained sprawled across the cracked floors. A reek of burned food made me wrinkle my nose. "You must visit Earth again."

"When will it be enough?"

"When it's enough," she replied, her eyes far away, her hands twisting in *The Cat's* fur.

"What's wrong?"

She faced me, a tension crossing her cheeks I hadn't noticed before.

"That's not for me to say."

"But if something is troubling you...You know I would do anything to help." I frowned at *The Cat*, as if it was his fault.

She took my hand in both of hers. "I know. But this time, the puzzle is all yours."

"What does that mean?"

"Only that you have a journey ahead of you."

Possibilities raced through my mind. Had I done something to upset her? Had I not granted the right dreams or chosen the correct mortals to visit? Was she unhappy here in my company in this vast and crumbling palace? After all, an eternity was a long time.

"Are you not content with your life here?" I dared to ask. I braced myself for her answer. If she wanted to leave, of course I would permit her.

"Of course I'm happy here," she replied, reaching out to pick up *The Cat*, who immediately nestled into her. "I'd never want to be anywhere else."

The relief of her words made my shoulders droop. I sighed. What was it then?

"Dreams aren't just for mortals," she said as she stroked *The Cat*. The animal gave me a reproachful look, as if I was missing something obvious.

I stared at Marguerite. It was my job to rule over Dreamland, to ensure that mortals' dreams were fulfilled, to control the level of their nightmares. It would continue to be my job for eternity. I had none of my own ambitions. No dreams. No fantasies. I wasn't permitted to marvel. But I wondered what Marguerite dreamed of.

"What is it you want, Marguerite...?" My hand floated to my chest where a dull ache settled between my ribs. Heartburn. Perhaps the food had spoiled. "Because if I have denied you something, if there is something you crave, please speak up."

"I have everything I need," she replied, dipping her

head toward *The Cat* and laying a gentle kiss on its furry head.

"What about what you want?"

"I have that too."

"Then what is it?"

Her eyes roamed my face, the intensity of her gaze setting my skin on fire.

"All in good time," she said, as she put *The Cat* back on the balcony and produced a new file from the air. "It's time for you to visit Lucius."

"A man?" I hadn't expected that. So far it was only women's fantasies I had been granting.

"Men have dreams too," Marguerite said, swatting me with the file.

"Of course they do." I moved out of the lowering sun and leaned against a broken column. "What is it Lucius dreams of?"

"Love," she said simply.

"Love? That's an easy one."

"Is it?" she asked as she pressed the file into my hands. I scanned the pages inside. He ran, he skied, he visited far-off places. It was a good life.

"He has so much," I said.

"But not the one thing he truly desires." Marguerite turned to face the land, her eyes roaming the blooming growth. "He'd give it all up for a shot at love."

I snapped the file closed and placed it on the balcony in front of Marguerite. The pages fluttered in a breeze. "I can grant him that. Mortal love is...easy enough. And perhaps, like Samantha Morris, his dream might come true."

"Perhaps," she said as I gathered my coat around me. "You'll need extra sand. He keeps his emotions guarded. He's not one to easily trust."

"Noted," I murmured as I disappeared in a sandy cyclone, my last glimpse of my world Marguerite's fiery hair.

Chapter Eight

SANDMAN

I ARRIVED on earth in the late afternoon. A wintry day with the sun falling early. People rushed along the sidewalks in the busy city, heads down against the wind. Lights popped on, illuminating human activity within. Did they know they were being watched?

I spotted a woman talking on a phone, sitting on an armchair, laughing. A man cooking in his kitchen, whipping a towel at a couple of giggling teenagers. An elderly woman with a cat curled on her lap. White. Like *The Cat* in Dreamland. They seemed happy enough, but why weren't they dreaming?

With my head tucked into the collar of my coat, I marched into the business district of the city, running through my words in my mind. Lucius was clever. He wouldn't fall for an eloquent speech.

I entered the modern skyscraper in New York's financial district and entered an impressive lobby decorated with polished floors and gilded mirrors. It reminded me a little of home.

Using a dusting of sand to make the receptionist compliant, I walked past her to the elevators and rode to the top floor. When I reached the uppermost level, I stepped out of the cab to find a secretary behind a large desk situated just outside Lucius' office. Mid-thirties, tied back brown hair, reading glasses perched on her nose. A studious attractiveness oozed from her as she peered at a computer screen.

I made it to Lucius' office, my hand on the door, before she looked up.

"You can't go in there." She half stood, a frown wrinkling her smooth brow.

I smiled. "It's okay, he's expecting me."

Her frown deepened as she stood. "There's nothing in his diary."

I blew a pinch of sand in her direction. "It's of a personal nature."

"Oh. Of course," she said as she sat back down and resumed her work.

I pushed the door open and closed it softly behind me. The penthouse office was large, with a triple aspect view of the city, but it wasn't elaborately decorated. A suite of comfortable furniture sat off to my left, a coffee table laden with magazines as a centerpiece. Behind it, the lights of a coffee machine and a small fridge glowed in the semidarkness. A rug connected the suite with Lucius' desk. The only light came from a lamp on the desk. Lucius sat under its glow in a leather chair, his back turned, his gaze trained on the city lights.

I cleared my throat.

Lucius turned. He locked eyes with me. "Did I miss an

appointment? I thought Abigail said my diary was clear. Enough time to prepare for the ceremony."

"Ceremony?" I asked as I approached his desk.

A flicker of unease crossed his handsome face. "I'm receiving an award."

He didn't elaborate. I didn't ask. I wasn't here for that.

"Congratulations," I said as I settled into one of the two chairs in front of his desk.

"Are you here for the presentation?" he asked, resting his elbows on the table and steepling his fingers. I looked at him, the rugged stubble lining his jaw, the expensive suit that fit him like a glove, the sadness in his eyes he couldn't hide. Not from me.

I smiled. "I'm here for you."

He pressed his palms against his desk, half rising. "If you're one of those reporters—"

I raised a hand. "Nothing like that. I'm a friend."

He sat again and opened a drawer in his desk. Did he keep a gun in there? Perhaps I'd have to use my sand sooner than I thought. "I don't know you."

"What is it you want, Lucius?" I asked, keeping my tone light and reassuring.

He stopped rummaging in the drawer and rested his hands on the table. "I don't understand."

"It's a simple question."

"Is it?"

I chuckled. "Perhaps not."

We stared at each other, sizing each other up. What would it be like to live on earth? To be on the cover of Time Magazine? To be one of the most eligible bachelors in the country, and yet to have found no genuine connection? Sad. Lonely. He'd given up on his dreams months ago. But it didn't prevent his success.

"Love is a nebulous thing," I said. "Hard to qualify. Difficult to explain. Almost impossible to recognize."

"What would you know of it?" he asked, pulling at his cuffs.

I tilted my head. "Nothing, as it turns out. I am not at liberty to experience true love."

"Who *are* you?"

"The Sandman."

He raised an eyebrow. Amusement trickled across his lips. "That's just a children's story."

"Is it?"

He laughed and settled back in his chair, resting his folded hands across his stomach.

"What is it you want, Lucius?"

"If you truly are The Sandman, wouldn't you already know?"

"I do," I said, leaning forward. "But sometimes it helps to clarify your wishes if you say them out loud. I cannot grant something vague and tenuous."

"You're not a genie."

"No, but I can allow you to experience your wildest dreams. At least while you're asleep."

"But then I'd wake up even more disappointed when I realized it wasn't real."

"Or perhaps you would be motivated."

He stared at me. "You see, that's the thing about love. No matter how motivated you are to find it, it doesn't make it happen."

I stood and walked around the desk. After perching

on the edge of his desk, I laid a hand on his shoulder. He didn't refuse the contact. "I don't want you to give up hope. If you lose hope..." I shook my head. There was no point telling him about the status of Dreamland. That was not his problem. "If you lose hope, then what is the point?"

I didn't allow him to answer. Instead, I blew a handful of sand in his direction. He fell asleep immediately. Standing, I watched him for a few moments. His eyes moved under his closed eyelids, his dreams already beginning.

As I made for the door, a tightness in my chest made me catch my breath. In all my years of ruling over dreams, I'd believed I was doing good. Giving dreamers access to their true desires. But what if I wasn't? What if Lucius was right? What if they woke up disappointed? How could I be responsible for that?

Chapter Nine

LUCIUS DEVILLE

LUCIUS STARED out the window at the twinkling city lights, wondering how the hell he could get out of the awards ceremony that night. It was his one-year anniversary with his wife and the last thing he wanted to do was smile and nod for the camera, play the political game with the powers that be, make small talk with private equity houses that only wanted him to throw an investment their way.

They would celebrate properly tomorrow night, but still the inconvenience grated. But if he didn't attend the ceremony, when everyone knew he was in New York, there would be rumors. Rumors didn't work well in his line of business, and he couldn't afford for people to cast aspersions in his direction. He had plans. For his wife. To give her everything she'd ever wanted. Because that's what she had done for him. Found him when he was drowning. Shown him that his future could be bright. That all his success could mean something.

He sighed when his office door opened, expecting his

personal assistant to be bringing in the entourage of make-up artists who would make him look presentable for the cameras. But when he turned, he saw his wife standing in the threshold.

Sofia, dressed in the most stunning red gown he'd ever laid eyes upon, stole his breath. It was her best color, complimenting her complexion, and making her stand out in a sea of black and other muted colors. Her long blonde, and usually unruly hair, was swept up in an elaborate do that made her look like a movie star of times gone by. The red dress covered her breasts modestly, but the back was low, revealing the slight curve of her well-shaped ass. The dress trailed to the floor, material puddling around her feet, only revealing the points of two red shoes.

"You look beautiful," he said when he found his voice. The desire to fuck her right then and there was almost too much to bear.

She smiled and gave him a mock curtsey. "You're winning an award for Businessman of the Year, I had to look the part."

"I wouldn't care if you turned up in a paper sack."

She approached him and fixed the collar of his shirt, her warm fingers trailing across the back of his neck. "You need to have higher expectations."

"You give me everything I need," he said, circling his hands around her waist.

He couldn't believe she was his. This exquisite creature who seemed to love him. They'd met over drinks in a bar. Lucius never normally attended bars, felt they were for the younger generation, but this particular client had insisted on a more casual meeting. So, gritting his teeth, he'd left his office and headed for the bar downtown, surprised to find Sofia as a member of the team he was meeting. He couldn't take his eyes off her the entire night and signed on the dotted line before they'd finished their spiel. Perhaps that had been their intention. He didn't care.

He woke the following morning, full of regret for not getting her phone number. But when going through his phone to frequent himself with his morning schedule, he found a breakfast appointment scheduled with her name and number. The smile that widened his face made him feel like a horny teenager. He called her immediately, and they had breakfast together that morning. They hadn't been apart since.

Now, in his office, while Sofia fussed over his appearance, he held her tight against his chest and pressed his nose into the hollow of her neck. Her smell drove him crazy, made all thought leach from his mind, made his desire harden into a wanton thing.

"Abigail arranged an entire team. They'll be here any minute…" he murmured into her hair.

"I canceled them," Sofia said. "I prefer you without make-up and bronzing powder."

Surprised, Lucius took a step back. "What are you doing here, then? I thought we were meeting at the ceremony?"

A wicked smile spread across Sofia's face. "I know you were disappointed we couldn't celebrate our anniversary properly tonight. But I thought we could steal a few moments to ourselves."

His heart thrummed in his chest. How was it possible for her to know him so well? "What did you have in mind?"

With one finger centered in his chest, she pushed him backward toward his desk, her eyes flashing with desire. He grew hard immediately.

"Sit," she commanded.

He sat. "We don't have time for this...we have to be across town in an hour and it's going to take—"

"Shush," she said, pushing him into his chair.

He shut up. Hell, he didn't want to go to the award ceremony anyway. Who gave a fuck if he was late? He could skip the dinner entirely. The award wouldn't be presented until after the dessert course. And the food was likely to be terrible anyway. And it's not like they could present the award without him, was it?

He smiled at his wife.

"That's better," she said, placing a knee between his legs, pressing against his straining erection. She yanked at his tie, pulling him forward, then lowered her head to kiss him.

Resting his hands on her waist, Lucius drew her tongue into his mouth, wrapping his own around it, probing her warmth and taste. Exquisite. She always tasted so exquisite. He'd waited five dates to kiss her, but it had been worth it. The best kiss of his life, as well as every single one that came after.

Lucius groaned. "What are you doing to me?"

"Turning you on, I hope." She placed a hand between his legs, testing the firmness of his dick.

She worked her hand over him, gently stroking,

making him even harder. So hard he could barely contain his need in his trousers. "What did I do to deserve you?"

He pulled her onto his lap, cupped her cheek, and ran his tongue along her jaw.

"I'm the lucky one," she said. She didn't know how wrong she was. She grinded against him, bucking her hips against his hardness, making him hungry and desperate.

Kissing his cheek, his lips, his ears, then his throat, she dropped to her knees.

"What are you doing?" he asked as she ran her hands along the inside of his thighs.

"I thought you deserved a special treat."

He put his hand over hers where it cupped his erection. "You don't have to." He moved to lift her back into his lap.

"Lucius," she said, with a hint of a reprimand. "I can't count the number of times you've gone down on me. Let me return the favor."

"But I enjoy going down on you," he said. "You taste like honey."

"And I enjoy pleasuring you."

Doubt crept into his thoughts. He'd spent so long without a relationship. Without love. Without even a glimmer. And then he'd walked into the bar that night, tired and weary from long days of presenting a façade, from long nights at the office. Where the hell else was there to spend his time? The ski slopes were empty without a partner. The cabin was cold without companionship. The yacht felt isolated when it was just him on the empty blue seas. What was the point without someone to share it with?

Then he'd walked into that bar and his eyes had immediately found hers. That was it. The thunderbolt struck, and he knew.

Sofia unfastened his trousers, dug her hands inside, and released his ripe erection. He groaned as her touch drifted over his shaft, beginning with gentle strokes.

"Just relax," she said, as she took him in her mouth.

He eased back in the chair, lifting his hips so she could take more of him into her mouth. Her warmth surrounded him, her teeth gliding gently over his length, her tongue working miracles at his throbbing head.

Tension built at the base of his penis, pulsing along his shaft, spasming with each movement of her tongue and teeth.

He clung to her shoulders. "I'm going to come."

She pulled away, a draft of air teasing his nakedness. "That would be the point."

Using the tip of her tongue, Sofia made circular motions up and down the length of his shaft. A small, breathless moan escaped his lips. He ached for her. Sofia took him in her mouth again, her lips encircling his throbbing cock, her teeth grazing his shaft, her tongue tying loops around his hard point. She relaxed her throat, taking more of him in, tantalizing him with sensation. He gripped the back of her head.

His eyes slid closed. Images of the two of them over the last year filled his mind. When they were home alone, rarely did they dress, but enjoyed each other's nakedness. Clothes were barriers to love. A nuisance when the need took them, which was often. He had explored every inch of her body, and still it enticed him to dizzying heights.

Sofia yanked his trousers to his knees. He didn't complain, and allowed her hands to circle his butt. Her fingers pressed close to his crack, and he clenched it closed. She squeezed his cheeks, urging him to loosen up. He couldn't say no to her. The pressure built in his iron-hard cock. Her mouth drove him crazy.

She pushed a finger past his clenched cheeks, circled his asshole, then pushed inside. His teeth slammed closed, and he bucked against her. No one had ever penetrated him in that way before. He was all set to throw her off when her finger dove deeper and a new sensation unlocked inside him. He gasped. The gasped turned to a roar. He gripped her shoulders as spasms pummeled his body. No longer a centralized location, but the pleasure spreading from his penis and anus in all directions.

His cock throbbed, his body spasmed. His warm seed sped through his shaft and into Sofia's mouth. She swallowed every drop as he pulsed inside her, letting out a roar he couldn't contain. Only she could make him feel that way. Uninhibited.

She removed her finger and pulled away to look at him.

"That was a surprise."

"I was saving that one," she replied with a purr.

"Sofia," he whispered her name as she climbed onto his lap, his erection showing no signs of abating.

She kissed him hard, sharing his taste. He didn't

mind. Mingled with her own flavors, it was a heady combination.

"I love you," he said.

She circled her arms around his neck. "And I love you."

He smiled at the thought of the roses she would find at home later. He'd bought out three florists in the neighborhood and had organized a delivery of one hundred bouquets of red roses. They were currently filling the house, the sweet fragrance of love possessing the air. And then there were the petals. A trail of red petals that led from the door to the bedroom and covered their white sheets. They would make love on the petals. Later. When they got home. And that was only the start. He had a dozen more surprises planned.

Sofia climbed off his lap. "Come on, or we'll be late."

He tucked his erection back into his boxer shorts, cursing the time he'd have to wait until he could take her again. After straightening his clothes, he took her hand, the smell of sex still strong in the air. He led her to the basement where his motorbike was parked and offered her the second helmet.

She didn't hesitate to put it on, then pulled up her long dress and straddled the saddle. Lucius glimpsed her sheer red panties. How he wanted to touch her there. To make her so wet, she'd beg him to take her, to make her scream.

Attempting to ignore his swollen cock, he swept a leg over the bike and gripped the handlebars, revved the engine into life. Sofia's arms circled his waist, grasping tightly, two fingers on her right hand dangling lower, teasing his desire.

As the bike shot out of the garage, he let out a roar of frustration. Already, he needed to be satisfied again. It took them only ten minutes to weave through the city traffic and reach the fancy museum. They arrived in time for the main course. Lucius made small talk, nodded and commented when appropriate, all the time trying to ignore the way Sofia's foot stroked his crotch.

He choked down dessert. Only half rose for the toast, considering he had nothing to hide his erection with. Sofia walked to the stage to present his award, her skin glowing, her hair tumbling loose, his need for her growing. Knowing he would be called to stage imminently, he thought of his dead Grandma and prayed his erection would go down.

The presentation of the award happened in a blur. Lucius hid his lower half behind the podium, made some half-assed speech that they all gathered close to hear. A few camera snaps. Another half hour of shaking hands and patting backs, then he was out of there. Practically dragging his wife out of the building, giving her a look that would leave her with little doubt as to his intention.

"What's the rush?" she laughed.

He chucked the tacky glass award in the saddle holder, wondering if it would survive the journey, not really caring if it did.

"Wait until I get you home," he growled.

She held him tight as they sped through the streets, his focus on the roads minimal, his mind and body only on her.

When they pulled up to their house twenty minutes later, he turned off the engine. Finally, everything slowed down. He didn't want a quick fuck. He didn't want to rush this. He wanted their first year together to mean something.

Lucius stood beside the bike, jangling the keys in his hand.

Sofia touched his arm, causing a tingling warmth to pool beneath her hand. "Are we going inside?"

"We are." Lucius cupped her elbow and guided her to the front door. The air was filled with the sweetness of roses.

Sofia unlocked the door, threw off her heels before she stepped inside, then gasped.

She turned to face him. "What's all this?" She indicated the bouquets of roses that filled every room, the trail of petals on the floor.

"For you," he said simply, cupping her cheek and kissing her deep. She melted in his arms, so he picked her up and carried her through the house, not bothering to turn on a light.

When they reached the master bedroom, moonlight spilled through the open curtains. Splashes of red dominated every surface. The rose petals were scattered over the bed, strewn across the carpet, dotted on the furniture, and even floated in the bathtub.

"It's beautiful," Sofia said, finding her feet.

"As are you," he said, keeping an arm around her until she was steady. He pushed a lock of her hair behind her ear, then kissed her again, luxuriating in her taste, feeling an ache build between his legs. He wanted her. He always wanted her. But not yet.

Lucius sat on the bed and watched his wife. Watched her take in the extent of the flowers, sniff the sweet air, fiddle with the items on her vanity. Laughing, she collected the petals in one hand and threw them into the air, letting them drift to her bare feet.

"No one has ever done anything like this for me," she whispered, a tear streaking down her cheek.

Lucius' chest tightened. "It was supposed to make you happy."

She wiped the tear away. "I am happy."

Sofia stretched, her long, elegant arms a ballerina pose over her head. Then she pulled the clips out of her hair, her long locks falling loose. The smell of her shampoo mingled with the scent of roses. Nothing had ever smelled so right. So sweet. So delicious. If he could bottle it, he'd make himself a fortune. Another one.

Lucius sat back on his elbows, watching her, the bulge in his pants straining at the seams. It was a brutal ache, filled with both anticipation and agony. One he enjoyed every time. "I never want to go back to the office. I want to stay here, in this room, with you, for the rest of my life."

She smiled. "Deal."

"Now, get naked."

Her smile turned salacious. "Anything you say."

She pushed the straps of the dress off her smooth shoulders. It slipped down her body and pooled around her bare feet, leaving her in only a red lace G-string.

"Jesus," Lucius muttered through clenched teeth. He was barely in control of herself.

Sofia cocked a playful finger at him. "There's no Jesus here, but you might well see God when I'm through with you."

Lucius had a flash of her from last Saturday morning, wearing nothing but one of his work shirts, a pencil used to tie up her hair, another in her hand, doing the New York Times crossword. He'd never been able to complete one. But Sofia did it every Saturday. Beauty *and* brains. He'd hit the jackpot. He could die happy. Right now. Well, maybe not now. Maybe after tonight, and a few more, and after they'd started a family, and after the kids were grown...*Stop thinking, Lucius.*

Sofia brought her hands up to her graceful neck, cradling her chin, cupping her aroused breasts with her arms, revealing a cleavage he wanted to bury himself in.

Lucius yanked at the bow tie currently strangling his neck and threw it across the room. Next were the cufflinks, which he tried to deposit on the bedside table, but they fell to the floor. Once his jacket was off and thrown across the room in the general direction of a chair, he pushed himself back on the pillows and stared at his sexy wife.

Her beauty had attracted him first. The long unruly waves of blonde. The piercing blue eyes that were only ever filled with love and warmth, and a devastating intelligence. The milky smoothness of her skin that he would spend hours stroking when he should have been asleep. The pull of her sensuous mouth that made it impossible to look her in the eyes when she was talking.

The curve of her neck begged for his lips, and he

kissed her there more often than anywhere else. At least when she had clothes on.

His eyes dropped to the mounds of her breasts, the aroused nipples hardening in a shaft of moonlight. Sofia rubbed rose petals across her breasts, leaving a trail of their scent, arousing her tight buds even more. He ached to touch her, but he wanted to draw out this night for as long as possible.

He glanced at her taut stomach, the slip of red material hiding the apex of her legs. How he longed to lower his lips to the warm folds between her thighs.

Sofia stuck two fingers into the lace of her panties and moved the material down her supple thighs, past her knees, past the delicate curve of her ankle.

His eyes fixated on the area between her legs. There were so many things he wanted to do to her. "Come here."

She obeyed immediately, sauntering to the bed. She crawled onto the mattress, working her way up his legs, her breasts skimming his feet, then his trousers, then his belt, then his shirt.

She straddled him. His trousers were the only barrier keeping him in check. His need pressed against the seams, the strain threatening to undo him. He touched her warm skin, drew lazy circles on her butt, stroked the smoothness of her back.

She settled on top of him, little movements driving his throbbing cock to new heights. The smell of her arousal mingled with the roses. Slowly, he traced a line across her back, around her hip, along the inside of her thigh, to her pulsing, wet mound.

She gasped and threw her head back.

He touched her clitoris with deft fingers. Slowing at first, teasing her, then with a practiced movement and speed, making her cries come closer together. She bucked against him, tightening her thighs around his shaft. He groaned, barely able to hold on, and he wasn't even naked yet.

He removed his fingers before she came, and she looked at him with murderous eyes.

"You bastard," she hissed, her hand clenching his penis. "I was almost there."

He grinned. "You're going to have to wait a little longer."

He sat up and flipped her onto her back. Petals flew into the air as she landed on the bed, legs already spread. He kneeled and parted her wider with his knee, pressing his thigh against her clitoris.

Sofia gasped, murmured his name as her eyes slid shut.

"Look at me."

She opened her eyes again and smiled. "Happy anniversary."

He spread her legs wider, then kneeled lower so he could cup her backside and spread her apart. He lifted her hips a couple of inches into the air. Her eyes slid closed again, but this time, he didn't mind.

"Lucius," she murmured as he kissed the inside of her thigh.

He started at her knees, kissing and licking and moving his tongue closer to the cleft between her legs, but never quite reaching. He wanted to drive her out of her mind. Ignoring his own aching bulge, his only thoughts were in pleasuring his wife.

"Please, Lucius," she begged, her hands reaching for him.

He moved his lips to the center of her sweet warmth, eliciting another gasp from his wife.

"Yes," she murmured as she arched her hips.

His tongue delved into her delicate softness, making her buck forward. He kissed her clitoris, drawing it into his mouth, his tongue working to devour the wet mound. Then he licked the line of her silken folds, allowing his tongue to dive deeper each time. Sofia writhed on the bed, her hips jerking, searching for contact. He gripped her tightly, keeping her still, as he worked his tongue over the point of her swollen need, kissing her most tender flesh and dipping into her drenched center. So wet. So ready.

Her muscles twitched around his tongue. Her body bucked out of his tight grip. She placed a hand on each side of his head and tugged him closer. He kneaded her clitoris with his tongue, pushed into her quivering depths, biting and licking and sucking until she couldn't remain still. Her gasps became one long cry of release. Her body bucked and spasmed. Her fingers tightened around his ears, and she cried out his name.

She fell back against the bed. "Jesus fucking Christ," she panted. "How did you get so good at that?"

He crawled up the bed to be level with her, kissed her deeply. "I was just born that way," he chuckled. "And I'm not done with you yet."

Sofia flipped to her knees. She tore off Lucius' shirt,

buttons spraying everywhere. Then she yanked down his trousers and his boxers, finally releasing his erection.

"Damn straight, we're not done," she said as she swept a leg over him.

She wrapped her fingers around his shaft. Lucius gritted his teeth so he wouldn't release too soon. Sofia raised herself to her knees, hovering over his throbbing head. He could feel the warmth radiating from her wet center, her muscles still pulsating.

Slowly, agonizingly slowly, she guided his penis into her warm depths. Lucius let out a long breath as she settled on top of him, taking his entire length and girth.

She rested her hands on his chest while he placed his on her hips. She started with slow movements, her hips circling gently, building the pressure. Lucius guided her in the rhythm he liked, feeling the pressure build along his shaft. Nothing had ever felt so glorious. Her warmth engulfed him, her muscles tensed and relaxed, driving him to the brink more than once. The feel of his cock inside her almost sent him over the edge. There was nothing better.

As she circled her hips, she gripped at his flesh with her fingernails and he tightened his hold on her hips, minimizing any gaps, filling her completely.

Her movements quickened and he couldn't take her eyes off her swaying breasts as she thrust against him, edging him closer to breaking point. Little moans escaped her mouth.

Sofia's muscles locked around his shaft, tightening until he throbbed with an exquisite pressure. The release surged through him and he thrust into her as he ejaculated.

Her cry came at the same time, making her hips circle more viciously, prolonging his own erection and orgasm, making him sit up and bite into her shoulder. She crushed his head to her chest, her hips bucking as the scream tore out of her mouth and filled the rose-scented air.

She collapsed against him, with him still inside of her, still pulsing, still throbbing.

"I love you," he said as she slipped down to the bed beside him.

"And I love you." She kissed him. "Congratulations on your award."

Lucius had almost forgotten about the damn award. Where had he left it? In the bike's saddle?

He woke with a start. His office was dark, the only light from the dim lamp on his desk. The city lights below seemed to mock him. All those people below, rushing in and out of restaurants and bars. Having fun.

With his head still stuck in the dream, he stood. A ball of disappointment lodged in his throat. It was the best dream he'd ever experienced. That overwhelming sense of love. Now it leached from his body, pooled at his feet, and dripped through the hardwood floor. It left behind only a muted anguish. The futileness of yearning for something he could never have. He wished he'd never woken up.

Checking his watch, he realized the award ceremony had started. They'd be halfway through the main course by now. A flush of anxiety heated the back of his neck as he thought about letting people down. Then he realized he didn't care. Leaving his office, he straightened his tie and took the elevator to the first floor.

Before the doors opened, he shook out his arms and gave himself a little pep talk, practiced his most charming smile. The one he'd used on the cover of Time Magazine. It seemed to fool them. But it didn't fool him when he looked in a mirror. He could never escape the pool of sadness in his haunted eyes. He had everything most people dreamed of in a million lifetimes, but he didn't have what he craved.

When he arrived at ground level, he was disappointed to see he didn't really own a motorbike. His driver drove him through the city streets to the fancy museum where the ceremony was taking place. After climbing out of the car, he mounted the stone steps, taking them quickly, in a hurry but not rushing.

He was greeted with smiles and handshakes. Everyone knew who he was. A champagne flute was thrust into his hands. Real crystal. He took a sip, savoring the expensive taste, wishing it tasted of Sofia's mouth. Or her dripping cunt.

The maître d' led him to his table, where he apologized for his lateness. No one seemed to mind. It was only a moment later when the lights dimmed and a spotlight revealed a stage.

"To present the award for Businessman of the Year, I give you Sofia Thompson."

The name startled him. He plucked the cloth napkin from his empty dinner plate and tightened it around a hand. A shadow walked on stage, then the spotlight framed her.

Lucius' breath caught. Time seemed to stop. Noise faded to the background. All he could see was her. Sofia. His Sofia from the dream.

"Lucius DeVille," she announced with a welcoming smile.

He hadn't even heard the preamble. He rose to his feet, totally out of control of his own movements, and somehow found his way to the stage. Jogging up the steps, he plastered his charming smile on his face, but this time, it was edged with hope.

As he approached Sofia, their eyes locked. They stared at each other as the applause died down. Without words, she pressed the glass trophy into his hands. A tacky thing, but he didn't spend long examining it. He had eyes only for her.

"Thank you, Sofia," he said softly, taking her hand and raising it above their heads.

She laughed, caught up in the moment, her long blonde hair tumbling loose, the exquisite red dress highlighting her beauty.

He turned to face the audience, knowing his dreams had finally come true.

Chapter Ten

SANDMAN

I RETURNED to Dreamland to find the palace completely repaired. The marble floors shone, the gilded ornaments glistened in reflected sunlight. Fountains provided soothing background noise, while angels played harps in the clouds, their joyous tears collecting in my containers to be turned into sand. The palace gardens were once again green, flowers blossoming from every corner. Hummingbirds flew from shrub to shrub, and brightly colored fish swam in the ponds.

Approaching my favorite balcony, I rested my hands on the cold stone. There were no fires. No volcanoes. No storms. No raging oceans. Everything was calm. There were still fields of dying grass, withered trees, shallow lakes, empty streams, but my lands were flourishing once more. It was all I cared about. My lands. Mortals' dreams. And yet a great emptiness grew in my chest. I found I could not smile.

"Another dream come true," Marguerite said as she joined me on the balcony.

"Is it?" I asked, unable to look at her.

"What's wrong?" she asked.

Gathering my thoughts, I stared at my feet. Black boots. Everything I wore was black. A mysterious color. A comforting color. The only hint of darkness in Dreamland.

"I fear Lucius may have been right."

"Lucius just met his future wife."

"But when he woke from the dream..." My eyes heated. I had never cried before.

Nothing had ever moved me to. Something had changed. "Did you not feel his pain?"

"It was only temporary," Marguerite said.

I shook my head. "It could have been much longer."

"It could have," she agreed quietly.

"I'm not sure I believe in what I'm doing anymore," I admitted, hoping the gods who I hadn't seen for centuries and who'd tasked me with this eternal role were truly gone.

"You bring people hope."

"Only to have it dashed the moment they open their eyes."

"They have to have dreams," Marguerite insisted.

"Do they?" I turned to face her, my gaze resting on the smattering of freckles that bridged her nose, the shape of her delicate ears, the fire of her hair. "It seems dreams bring only despair."

"That's not true," she whispered, her hands trembling. She plucked *The Cat* from the balcony and clutched it to her chest. "Look at your land. Look what you have created. You've brought back hope. Mortals are dreaming again."

I stuck my hands into my pockets, feeling the reassuring grains of sand filter through my fingers. "It's not enough."

"You're not a god," Marguerite said. "You can't make all their dreams become a reality. That would be..." she nibbled on her lower lip. "Chaos."

"And who's to decide whose dreams come true and who's do not?"

"Not you. That's not your job."

I snorted my disdain, but remained silent. These new alien thoughts sent a heavy anxiety through my limbs. I'd never questioned my job before, but visiting the mortals had made me see something differently. I rarely visited earth. Only once or twice before, out of pure curiosity. This past week I'd been there more times than all the centuries before.

Now, the grittiness of their lives had rubbed off on me. The strength they fought with to achieve their ambitions. The aspirations they carried even in the face of the darkest nights. But their dreams had faded.

"I don't know what my job is anymore," I said, blowing a handful of sand across my land. It flew through the air, swept through the clouds, settled on the angels and made their golden harps glisten. They smiled and sang to me with their sweet voices. But they were voices that no longer charmed me.

"To protect the dreams of mortals." Her answer came quickly, unequivocally, but it no longer sat right with me.

"What is it you want, Marguerite?" I had asked her this once before.

"I told you, I have everything I need."

Need. Not want.

"What is it *you* want?" she asked me.

"I'm not allowed to want anything." It was a lie. I did indeed have things I yearned for, but they weren't mine to claim. And not something I could admit to as the King of Dreams.

Marguerite didn't reply. Instead, she plucked a file from the air and pressed it into my hands. "Your next case." She turned and left, her heels clacking on the cold marble floors.

I watched her go, her red hair the last thing to disappear behind the white arches. When I could no longer hear her heels, I opened the file. I found the picture of a college student smiling back at me. Senior year. Acing her studies. Also a swimmer, breaking college records. She was a virgin. Something that shamed her. It made her turn down dates. She didn't want to disappoint the few guys who'd shown her interest with her inexperience. My heart ached for her lack of self-esteem. She didn't need sex; she needed confidence. But, as I'd said to Marguerite, it wasn't my job to change reality. I could only give mortals their desires within their dreams.

Chapter Eleven

SANDMAN

I TRAVELED to Earth once again. My sandy cyclone deposited me on a lush, green lawn in the middle of a sprawling university. All red bricks and slate roofing. Stained glass and old-fashioned quads.

It was late, approaching eleven o'clock as I stared up at the imposing library. I walked through the wide entrance doors, past the reception area, and into the library itself. Bookshelves lined every wall, towering until they reached the tall windows. Dark at this hour. It reminded me a little of the vast library back in Dreamland, such was its scope. Large oak desks with dim lamps were placed at regular intervals between stacks. A handful of scattered students worked at this hour, but most of the desks and aisles were empty.

I spotted Bethany immediately. Halfway down a row of desks, a stack of books beside her, furiously scribbling notes on a legal pad, dark curls spilling over her face. I smiled. She appeared to be at home in the hush of the library. Why did she want to concern herself with what others thought?

I nodded at the librarian, blowing her a hint of sand so she wouldn't interfere, then made my way slowly to Bethany. I cleared my throat as I approached, so as not to startle her, and pulled out the opposite chair. She didn't look up, but continued to scribble notes.

I leaned across the table, pressing my palms against the solid surface, and whispered, "Bethany."

She looked up with a start, a hand flying to her chest.

"I'm sorry," I said. "I didn't mean to startle you."

A ghost of a smile warmed her features. "Sorry, I was totally in my own world."

I gestured to her notes. "Is it interesting?"

"Very. I'm a psychology major. Humans fascinate me. The decisions they make, their motivations."

I wondered if she understood her own compulsions. Her own shame.

I mirrored her fragile smile. "Do you feel as if you're learning about yourself at the same time?"

Her smile dropped. "Who did you say you were?"

"I didn't."

She glanced left and right, perhaps checking to see if there were people she could call on for help.

I raised a palm. "I'm not here to hurt you. The opposite, in fact."

She cocked her head, inspected me down her delicate nose. "How so?"

"I want to grant you your wildest fantasy. For one night. In your dreams."

She laughed. Magic didn't exist on earth. Of course that was her reaction.

I smiled to show her I was genuine.

"And how the hell would you go about doing that?"

"You let me worry about the details," I said, toying with the sand in my pocket.

"Do you know what my wildest fantasies are?"

"I do," I replied.

She waited me out until I filled the silence. I was not particularly practiced at conversing with humans, only Marguerite.

"You are ashamed of your...virginity," I lowered my voice when I spoke the word. "You turn down dates because you fear people will mock you for your inexperience."

Her eyes glinted. I couldn't quite read the emotion. Had I embarrassed her?

"That's not it," she said, her tone as flat as steel.

I frowned. "That's not your desire? To lose your virginity?"

"No. I mean, yes. But that's not why."

"It's not?"

She shook her head.

"But the file said—"

"You have a file on me?"

"There is a file for every dreamer."

"Who *are* you?"

"I'm not a stalker, or anything creepy. I promise."

"Could have fooled me."

I blew some sand in her direction. She coughed and

rubbed a few grains out of her eyes, but at least it made her amenable.

"So tell me," I said, resting my chin on my hand. "What is your great desire?"

Bethany put down her pencil, gave me her full attention. "It's true that I do want to lose my virginity. But I want it to be—"

"Special?"

She tilted her head, considering. "I don't need to be in love, if that's what you mean, but I want it to be with someone experienced, who can show me the ropes. Someone I can trust. Bonus if they're attractive too." She looked around the library. "Most of the guys here are really not up to the task. You get a drunken fumble, and that's about it. According to my friends, anyway."

"I wouldn't know." I had never attended college. "Did you have anyone in particular in mind?"

She picked up her pencil and tapped it against her notepad. "Do I have to tell you that?"

"No, the dream will be whatever you want it to be. I don't need the details. But I must update your file. I'll let Marguerite know there's been an error. There's never been an error before..." I caught myself. "Sorry, you do not need to know the details."

"Sounds complicated."

"It's not usually."

We sat in silence for a moment. Was I doing the right thing, granting someone their wildest fantasy? What if she woke disappointed? But at least she would have knowledge of the act that made her so curious.

I shook my head. It wasn't my place to judge. To

decide what her dream should be. That was up to Bethany. I was only here to grant them.

"Are you ready for a nap?" I didn't wait for a reply, but blew another handful of sand in her direction. A moment later, her head dropped into her arms.

Chapter Twelve

BETHANY JAMES

BETHANY SNAPPED AWAKE, her head fuzzy, a pool of drool marking her notepad. *Classy.*

Her eyes felt grainy. As she wiped them, she reached for her thermos of coffee and took a swig, almost spat it out. Cold. Checking her watch, she realized she'd dozed off for over an hour. It was nearing midnight, and if she had any chance of making it to her 7am class the next day, she better get home and get to bed.

She packed up her things, shoved them in her backpack, and said goodnight to the librarian. Standing outside in the cooler night air, she stared at the campus security phone, contemplating calling for an escort to her dorm. Her room was only a ten-minute walk away, and she wouldn't have to leave the campus grounds. Even so, everyone knew about the dangers of campus rape. She did not plan on being a statistic.

Bethany checked her rape alarm, peered into the shadows. She could run it. Or maybe she should go back inside and snuggle up between the stacks.

"Hello," a voice said in her ear, making her jump five feet.

"Shit! Fuck! Shit!" She whirled around to face the voice, recognizing the friendly smile instantly. She collapsed her hands to her thighs and dragged in a few breaths to settle her heart. "Don't do that to me."

Professor Carrington raised his palms. "I'm so sorry. I didn't mean to frighten you."

"S'okay," she said, regaining her breath. "But just so you know, you really can't creep up on a woman like that."

He tipped her a mock salute. "Point taken."

"You're here late," Bethany said. She gave him a once over. Noted the beard was longer than usual, the blue eyes glassy, his hair a little wild. She liked it.

"Prepping for finals."

She took a step back, gave him a cocky grin. "Any clue to what's going to be on them? I'm assuming my favorite professor will want to give me a tiny hint."

He laughed, shook his head, mimed zipping his lips shut. "As much as I'd like to help one of my top students, no can do."

She pretended to pout.

"Besides, you don't need the help."

"Only because I pull all-nighters in the library." She pointed to the building.

Professor Carrington checked his watch. "You call this an all-nighter? Students today, such wusses."

She socked his shoulder. "Well, if I didn't have to worry about walking back to my dorm in the dark, I would have stayed later."

"Touché." He smiled. "Would you like me to walk with you?"

The relief leached from her shoulders. She'd no longer have to jog the ten minutes back to her room, keep to the shadows, inspect the rustling bushes. Or engage in the subsequent hour she'd have to spend deep breathing and practicing relaxation exercises just to get her heart rate back to normal.

"That would be great, thank you."

"No problem." He shoved his hands in his pocket, hunched against a chill in the air. "You're on my way home."

Bethany remembered Professor Carrington's house just off campus. He entertained a select group of students once a semester with a takeout and a few beers. It was a three-story townhouse. White, gray, and other neutral tones, the odd splash of color; navy blues and deep purples. Light and airy. A home she'd felt comfortable in. And it was just him and his dog.

They walked in silence for a minute, then Bethany plucked up the courage to ask the question that had been on her mind. "If I stay here to do my masters, I'm really hoping for that TA spot."

"I'm sure you'd get it," he said. His reply came quick and instant, causing a warm flush to spread over her skin. "That is, if you're sure you don't want to accept a place at one of those fancy East Coast colleges?"

"And not be taught by my favorite professor? Never."

They smiled at each other and somehow came to a stop halfway to the dorm.

"There's something else I want to ask you," Bethany said.

"Something besides what's on the finals?" he laughed.

"Yeah, besides that."

"Okay. Sure. Shoot."

"It's a little unconventional."

"I think I can deal with that."

"Okay, maybe *a lot* unconventional."

He leaned toward her and wiggled his eyebrows. "I'm intrigued."

She hesitated. What if he turned her down? Would their relationship be ruined? And she so desperately wanted to be his TA next year.

"Is everything okay, Bethany?"

She liked the way he used her full name. Everyone else just called her Beth.

"I like to think we have a good relationship, for a professor and student."

Professor Carrington rubbed the back of his neck, the first inkling that he was growing uncomfortable. Maybe she should quit while she was ahead, before it was too late. But fuck it, carpe diem and all that.

"I would agree." He scuffed the floor with a shoe.

"Maybe even more than a professor student relationship? That we're friends."

"That would be accurate."

She faced him square on. "Do you think we could level that up a notch? Just for one night?"

"I'm not sure I know what you mean."

"Oh, I think you do." She walked closer so their noses

were only inches apart, looked up into his striking blue eyes, felt his breath on her cheek.

"You're right, that *is* unconventional," he said, but he didn't step away. "I'm old enough to be your father—"

"Hardly."

He rubbed his face. "Aren't there any boys your age that you're interested in?"

Bethany rolled her eyes. "The boys my age are all immature jerks."

"We've talked about gross generalizations in statistics class—"

"We're not in class right now."

"No, I guess we're not."

Bethany took a breath. "It's like this. I'm a virgin. I'm not in love with anyone. I've decided I want to know what sex is like. And as most of the guys my age still don't know what they're doing, I want to find someone who's been around the block a few times—"

"Ouch."

"In a good way. Someone experienced. Someone I know. Someone I respect and trust. Someone who's not going to drink a beer and fall asleep on me."

"That bad, huh?"

"You would not believe it." She stared at him, bracing herself for a response.

"I don't know what to say."

"Say, yes," Bethany urged.

He looked at his feet, the distant library, the dark clouds scudding across the moon, then finally at her face. Was his heart beating as loudly as hers?

"It's really not appropriate. I don't want you to feel

like you've been taken advantage of, not to mention the fact that I could lose my job."

Bethany latched onto the positives. "So you're considering it?"

"You have made it a mission to worm your way into my heart."

"I promise it will be our secret. And in another ten days, it won't matter anymore, anyway."

"You're very determined."

"Surely you knew that about me already."

"I did."

"You can't say no."

"Can't I?"

She socked his shoulder. "You know you want to." She jutted a hip, gave him a little shimmy.

"Do I?" He grinned, and she knew she'd won. "What's in it for me?"

"A night of passion with yours truly."

"Thought you said you were a virgin and inexperienced?"

"Well, you see, I figure you can teach me all the wicked ways, mold me into the perfect sexual partner. What's not to love about that?"

"Tempting."

They continued walking. Bethany sensing her victory until they reached her dorm and he stopped outside the front door.

Professor Carrington leaned down and pecked her cheek. "Come see me after your last final. Then we'll talk."

God Dammit.

Bethany put down her pen, gathered her belongings, and raced out of the exam hall. There was only one place she wanted to go. She ran through the sunlit quads, across the lawn which had only recently been seeded, weaved through the dorm buildings, and out of campus.

She slowed down as she walked along the sidewalk, trying to catch her breath, knowing it was impossible to still her racing heart until she saw his face. But he'd promised. Once she'd finished her last final. That was today, now. Right this second. And she was determined to claim her prize.

Bethany stood outside the brick townhouse, readjusted her clothing, swept her fingers through her hair. She rang the bell, listened for footsteps. A dog barked. She remembered it was a blonde cocker spaniel, all wild, unruly hair. Owners really did look like their dogs, she mused. And in this case, both were highly attractive.

She heard his footsteps, then him clear his throat. A sudden pressure built between her legs. The anticipation of what was to come.

The door swung open. Professor Carrington stood in the threshold, no shirt, loose jogging bottoms, bare feet. She fixated on his abs. She'd had no idea he was hiding such an exquisite body beneath his work shirts. A taught six pack that narrowed to a finely tuned waist. A smattering of chest hair that matched the color of his beard.

She remembered to look at his face.

He leaned in the doorway, crossed his arms, smiled.

"Hi," she said, suddenly nervous.

His eyes twinkled with amusement. "I'm assuming you've come straight from your last final."

"I did."

"How did it go?"

"Fine."

"How did you find that last question?"

"I'm not here to talk about the exam."

He grinned. "No, I thought not."

"Can I come in?" Her heart thudded in her chest. Today she would finally know what it felt like to be with a man. Sure, she'd experienced orgasms, pleasured herself, but this would be a true connection. A meeting of minds as well as bodies.

"That depends. Are you here to use my body and leave the cash by the door on your way out?"

"You know it's not like that."

"As old and as experienced as you think I am, I'm not in the habit of a one night...or day...stand."

"What are you saying?" She inched backward, heat flushing her cheeks.

"Ever since you propositioned me ten days ago...I haven't been able to get you out of my head." He looked at his feet, reached down to pet the dog, who sat on his toes, then looked her right in the eyes. "Not that it hadn't crossed my mind before; you're beautiful, and smart, and determined. You've got a bright future in front of you."

"But?"

"There's no but."

"Thank God."

"I let myself feel. Realized what I'd been hiding from

myself, because I'm not the sort of teacher who would prey on a student. Not now, not before, not ever. Your proposition woke me up to my true feelings."

"True feelings?"

"Yes, my true feelings, Bethany." Her name sounded like treacle in his mouth. "I don't want to have sex with you...unless you see yourself in a relationship with me."

Her world spun. She'd never considered a relationship. Not with him. And not because she didn't have feelings, but because she thought he'd never go for someone like her.

She pushed past him into the house, shut the door. "Let's get to it then."

Without waiting for an invitation, Bethany walked up the stairs. She'd never been to the second floor before, and she was curious to see what his bedroom was like.

She heard him trailing behind her, muttering. "Jesus Christ, now I'm nervous. Haven't been this nervous since I was a teenager."

She smiled secretly to herself.

"It's this way." He passed her and led her along the hall to the end room. She opened the door to a burst of light. More neutral colors, a French balcony with wispy white curtains. Attractive prints of animals on the walls. A massive super king bed.

Bethany turned in a slow circle, taking it all in; the realization of what they were about to do finally dawning on her. Her lip trembled.

"Would you like a glass of wine? I have a nice red in the kitchen I could grab. Or if you prefer white, I can run out and get a chilled bottle—"

She walked up to him and pressed her fingers to his lips. "Shhh. Let's get this over with."

He frowned, held her arms. "It isn't something to get over. It's something to enjoy."

"I'm nervous."

"Do you trust me?"

"Yes."

"Then don't be nervous. I'll take care of you."

She wound her arms around his neck and pressed her lips against his, his beard tickling her chin.

"Professor Carrington?" she whispered around the edge of a kiss.

He pulled back, threw his head back, and laughed. "Okay, quit with the Professor bullshit. It's Steve from now on, okay?"

She smiled. "Okay, Steve."

He lifted her in his arms, kissed her again, his tongue probing her mouth. She felt him harden against her. Her own need intensified. She didn't know how long she could wait as the longing built between her legs, pulsing, throbbing, begging for satisfaction.

"Steve?" she murmured.

"Yeah?"

"Can I touch it?"

"Touch what?"

"Your penis."

He released her, kissed her cheek. "Sure."

Keeping her eyes on him, she stepped up close, pressed her hand against his straining erection. He groaned, slitted his eyes closed. "God, that feels good."

"I haven't done anything yet."

"I'm easily pleased."

"I'll keep that in mind."

She threaded her fingers into the waistband of his joggers, delving into the soft down of his curls, reaching for him. She wrapped her hand around his shaft, amazed at how it throbbed and strained in her hand. Steve groaned again, wrapped his arms around her, held her tight.

She looked at the shaft in her hand, the length, the girth. "I don't think that's going to fit."

He chuckled, his lips near her ear. "It'll fit."

She held on to him, gently touching, until he wrapped his hand around hers and showed her how to move her hand. Up and down, gentle strokes, a quickening pace. She wanted it inside her, but the feel of it in her hands, the size of it, the throbbing excitement, kept her in place.

"Wait," he growled, stopping her movements. "We're not here for this."

"We're not?"

"No, we're here for you to lose your virginity. And to be honest, I'm practically naked, and you're fully dressed. Let's even that up a bit, shall we?"

She giggled, suddenly shy, and dropped her hand from his pulsing hardness.

Steve kicked off his joggers, allowing Bethany to examine him in all his naked glory. The line of his firm jaw, the curve of his muscular shoulders, the breadth of his chest, the sculpted abdomen, the supple thighs, and his enormous erection. She couldn't take her eyes off it. Equal parts desire and fear thudded in the junction between her legs.

Staring directly into her eyes, he undid her cardigan, button by button, a reassuring smile creeping onto his lips. She slipped her arms out and let it fall to the carpet. Then his hands were on her T-shirt, tugging the waist out of her jeans, pulling it up over her head. The cool air rippled across her exposed skin.

Steve stared at her bra, a plain white T-shirt bra that she clearly hadn't thought through. He cupped a breast through the satin fabric and rubbed a thumb over her nipple. He kissed her shoulder, then her throat, let his lips trail down her chest until they paused at the sensitive area between her breasts.

"You are amazing," he muttered, slipping the straps of her bra from her shoulders.

A second later, the bra fell to the floor to join her cardigan. She stood in a shaft of sunlight, her breasts exposed, luxuriating in the weight of his lustful gaze.

Steve kneeled in front of her, kept his eyes locked on hers as he undid the buttons of her jeans. He shimmied the stiff denim down her legs, past her knees, until she could step out of them and kick them across the floor.

His warm hands roamed her body, cupped the swell of her breasts, stroked the flatness of her stomach, tickled the curve of her thighs. His fingers trailed upwards along her inner thigh until he reached her needful center. But he didn't touch. Not yet. He leaned back on his heels and let his eyes roam over her body. "You're so beautiful."

A heavy sensation pulsed through her vagina. She feared her knees would buckle at any moment and she would swoon and faint like an old-fashioned lady of a time from long ago. His scrutiny turned her on, made her impatient, intensified her desire.

"How far have you gone before?" he asked.

"Far enough, but never this," she murmured.

He gripped her buttocks, dug his fingers into her flesh, making her cry out. Then his face was near her hot and waiting center, separated by only the thinnest of materials. His warm breath gusted against her, inflaming her need, making her want to scream in frustration.

"Can we get on with it?" she begged.

"There's no rush," he said with a wicked grin.

He pressed a hand against her quivering mound, sending her crazy with desire. Then he kissed her through her panties. She gripped his shoulders.

He tore off her panties with his teeth and pressed his mouth to her clitoris. She leaned into him, putting some of her weight onto his face. His tongue darted inside her, his teeth nipped at her clit. She gasped as the desperate sensations consumed her.

Steve pushed her leg away, made her spread her legs apart, then dove deeper inside her waiting slit. His tongue brushed over her clitoris, delved deep between her folds, working inside her, kissing and licking and nipping, driving her to new heights of desire.

"Fuck me," she hissed. "Fuck me now. And don't give me that 'there's no rush' bullshit."

Steve laughed, got to his feet, and picked her up. He carried her to the bed and threw her onto the mattress. After rolling a condom onto his erect penis, he crawled across the bed.

Bethany lay on her back, spread her legs, willing him

to enter her. He lay on top of her, his weight balanced on his elbows, staring into her face, kissing her lips, her breasts, her throat. Each kiss left behind a tantalizing fire. She arched closer to him, wanting more, feeling his need press against her.

"Please," she begged.

"I can't take it anymore, either," he said.

With one hand, he guided his throbbing shaft to her waiting entrance, hovered there, stared into her eyes. "You okay?"

"I won't be if you don't get on with it."

He pushed his penis into her, just an inch, but it was enough to send a spasm pulsing through her body. She arched her hips to take more of him in, marveling that his girth actually fit inside her. But he wasn't all the way in yet.

He placed a hand behind her head, the other under her buttocks, lifting her to meet him. Another inch and he paused again.

"You're doing this on purpose." She bit his shoulder, showing him she meant business.

"I don't want to hurt you. I want your first time to be pleasurable."

"I don't care anymore," she groaned into his chest.

Another inch, then another, until he was all the way inside. He paused there, allowing her to adjust to his size. Her muscles tightened around him. She told herself to relax.

"You're so tight," he murmured, dropping his mouth to her breasts.

Bethany wrapped her arms around him, dug her

fingers into his buttocks, pulling him deeper, ready for more. "I'm okay."

Steve began tenderly, slowly, his thrusts gentle and even.

A snap of pain sliced through her, and then it was gone, and then there was only the sensation happening deep within her center. Her wetness coated him, spurring him on.

They laced their hands together, found a natural rhythm. Steve's breaths came in quick grunts. Bethany's pants matched.

"I don't know how long I can hold on," he said.

"Don't stop," Bethany murmured.

He didn't. He pounded into her. Harder, faster, filling her depth entirely. Filling her in a way she didn't know she could be filled. Sating a need that had been crying out for too long. She arched her back, lifted her hips to meet every one of his powerful strokes.

Her clitoris tingled with pleasure. Deeper inside, gentle spasms pushed through her depths. She clenched against him, gripping his back, pulling him deeper. His mouth on her breasts, his thrusts harder and faster. Until finally she came. The orgasm ripped out of her, spreading from deep within, through her limbs, making everything quiver with pleasure.

His even strokes matched her rhythm, drawing the orgasm out until she couldn't take it any longer. She bit down on his lip, muting the scream in her throat, riding the wave she never knew existed.

Beneath him, Bethany bucked and writhed, slammed her hips against his, begged him to keep going. He didn't stop. And as soon as the first orgasm faded, another one began.

She scraped at his back, yanked at his body, taking all of him she could. After the second orgasm tore through her, her mind going to a different place, her body barely able to contain the pleasure, she slipped out from underneath him and pushed him onto his back.

Straddling him, she took him back inside her, now dripping with the evidence of her pleasure. Bethany took his hands and placed them on her breasts. He crushed her breasts in his hands, tweaking her nipples. She circled her hips, faster and faster, until his eyes slid closed and his hands reached to grab her hips.

She continued the motion, sliding up and down his engorged flesh, drawing out his need to release. Then he tensed, his body going rigid, his hands clenching her hips. But she didn't stop. She rode him and she rode him hard. She contracted her muscles around him, feeling her own orgasm build once more. They came together, bucking against each other, wetness between them, the sound of their slick bodies filling the room. The release surged through her, creating a heated frenzy until his spasms inside her subsided and the uncontrollable shudders of pleasure ebbed away.

They clung to each other as the shudders abated, kissing and nipping, hands roaming each other's bodies. Finally, they were still, collapsing back in the bed to lie beside each other.

"Jesus H, why did I put that off for so long?" Bethany laughed.

"Because you needed to find someone like me." Steve draped an arm across her stomach.

"You got that right. I'll leave the money at the door, right?"

Steve sat bolt upright.

Bethany raised her palms. "Kidding!"

"Good," Steve said, settling himself back on the bed. "Because I think I'm a little bit in love with you, Miss James."

Bethany snapped awake, her head fuzzy, her eyes grainy. Getting her bearings, she rubbed her eyes and realized she was still in the library. A feeling of satisfaction hovered between her legs, even though she knew it had just been a dream. *But damn, that was one hell of a dream.*

As she gathered her books, Bethany spotted Professor Carrington on the other side of the library. Maybe she could ask him to walk her home. Maybe it would lead to something else. But she would never put him in that position while she was still his student. She wasn't the same Bethany as in her dream. Then again, if she didn't try, she'd never know.

Chapter Thirteen

SANDMAN

I RETURNED TO DREAMLAND, arriving in the magnificent marble hall to find Marguerite barefooted, wearing a flowery dress, and dancing to music that filled the palace. Hanging back in the shadows, I watched her sway to the alluring melodies. She glided across the floor, her arms moving above her head, her bare feet pirouetting effortlessly across the polished floor. My chest swelled with emotion as I noted the satisfied smile on her lips. She was happy.

She spotted me, startled. Stopped dancing. A gentle blush rose to her cheeks and she covered them with her hands. "I didn't know you were back."

"Just now," I said, walking toward her.

Her smile widened, stretched all the way to her pale blue eyes. She ran across to me and grabbed my wrist. "Wait until you see."

"See what?"

She dragged me to the balustrade, the one we often

stood at together, the one that gave us the best outlook of Dreamland.

"Look." She pointed.

I walked outside, raising my face to the morning sun, to find a changed land. A herd of unicorns ran through the wild meadows, biting at fruit from the plump orchard trees. Bees droned lazily in the air, bringing flowers of every color and size to full bloom. Forests rolled out in the distance, and beyond that a snowcapped mountain. Dreamers occupied the land. It was impossible to interact with them while they were here, riding pegasuses, or flying with the angels, or skiing down the mountains, or doing any number of magical things, but a dusting of my sand kept their dreams from turning sour.

"I have a surprise for you," Marguerite said. She hadn't let go of my wrist and tugged me down the stone steps, urging me past the iron table where I took my morning coffee, and into the manicured lawns surrounding the palace. Through the ornate gate at the end of the path, into the meadows brimming with wild-flowers.

"Where are we going?" I asked.

She only laughed in response.

The meadows turned into shadowy forests of towering sequoia, large apes and dreamers swimming from their branches, and still we walked on. Eventually, we emerged out the other side of the forest, arriving at a narrow sandy beach. It mantled a magnificent lake with a floating raft anchored a few yards out. On the sand lay a checkered picnic blanket and a basket bursting with food.

"I've never been here before," I said.

"It's new," she replied. "The library is filling up again with the dreams of mortals. This lake is new."

"It's beautiful."

"Which is why I thought it would be a great place to have a picnic. We have bread and cheese and champagne, and grapes and cakes and many wonderful morsels."

I hated to burst her enthusiasm. "If mortals really are dreaming again, I need to make more sand." It was a laborious process. While Marguerite reigned in the library and brought any problems to my attention, I spent most of my time in the palace cellar, grinding my sand from angels' joyous tears. That same sand would keep my pockets full, ensuring I never ran out.

"The sand can wait," Marguerite said, dipping a toe into the lake. "You deserve a moment to yourself."

I frowned. "Do I?"

She turned to face me, her eyes sweeping over me, taking in every detail. Could she see how tired I was? How confused?

"Of course you deserve to be happy."

"Happy," I repeated, the word unfamiliar in my mouth. "I thought I was here to perform a job."

"Is that all you want, after all this time?"

I didn't answer her, but wrestled with my thoughts. I didn't know how to make her understand the new yearnings inside, the ones I had buried deep. I couldn't be effective at my job if I gave in to my own whims.

"Let's eat," she said, gesturing for me to sit.

"Maybe for a minute," I said, kicking off my black boots. Her happiness was more important to me than the mortals. After all, she had been my assistant for decades, plucked from the mortal realm to live in Dreamland with me. There had been others before her, but she had lasted the longest, never seeming to grow tired of the job or my company.

"Take off your coat."

"But that's where I keep my sand."

She leaned over and pushed the coat from my shoulders.

"Loosen up a bit, Sandy."

I folded the coat neatly by my side. A cool breeze tickled the bare skin of my feet. I couldn't remember the last time I'd taken off boots or coat.

"You look so uncomfortable." She laughed, hiding it behind a hand.

I returned her smile, admiring the way the sun shone on her hair, her skin, her everything. She was a much better dream keeper than me.

"Here." She thrust a champagne flute into my hand. The bubbles fizzed to the top, intoxicating to watch. "I think that last dream cinched it."

"Another dream come true," I said. "But it could have all ended so badly."

Marguerite folded her legs underneath herself and sipped at her champagne. "You need to leave the pessimism behind."

"I like to think I'm being realistic."

She shook her head.

"Please don't mock me. I'm only trying to keep dreamers safe."

"I'm sorry. I didn't mean to imply..." She reached out a

hand to touch me, but I caught her wrist. Her touching me while I was in such a delicate state of mind would only evoke desires I couldn't act on. "I would never mock you."

A dark shadow burst over the sun and the temperature dropped suddenly, making Marguerite shrink. "There's a storm coming."

"We don't have storms in Dreamland. Not one's that interact with us, anyway." I frowned at the sky, the presentient of danger prickling the length of my spine.

It began to rain. Great big drops of water that splattered on our heads and faces. Getting to her feet, Marguerite turned her face to the sky and opened her mouth. "I love rain."

I caught a sense of movement, scanned the area for distressed dreamers, but could find only darkening clouds and flashes of lightning. "We should get inside."

"But the weather makes me feel so alive."

Ripples in the lake.

"Marguerite!" I launched to my feet.

With her back to the water, she didn't see the monster emerging from the lake. An enormous eel that erupted from the rippling surface and rose high into the sky. Two beady eyes focused on Marguerite and a large mouth gaped open, revealing countless rows of needle-sharp teeth.

"Marguerite!" I shoved my arms into my coat, dug my hand into a pocket, searching for my sand.

A noxious stench filled the air. The surrounding flowers leached of color. Lightning struck the lake, electrifying it, electrifying the eel. The jaws came down.

Marguerite turned. Her body trembled as she locked her eyes on the formidable beast.

I ran to her. As the jaws descended and as she dropped to her haunches, I swept an arm around her and brought her close. The enormous beast brushed past us, its breath making me gag. My hair stood on end as jets of electricity shot by, pricking at my skin, burning small holes in my clothing. The beast knocked us over, causing me to drop my sand.

Marguerite screamed, and a line of red opened along her torso. *No.*

I fumbled for another handful of sand. The beast prepared itself for a second attack, raising its mass to the sky, opening its wide jaws once more. Blowing my sand, I pictured the marble hall, and a second later we were teleported there.

I stood in the center of the great hall, listening to the distant thunder, holding a drenched Marguerite in my arms. Her eyes were closed, her body slack. Blood dripped from a wound at her waist.

"No, please, no." I shook her. "Marguerite. Marguerite, *please.*"

She remained slack in my arms. I carried her up a flight of steps, along a hallway and into my bedroom. Laying her on the bed, I grabbed towels from the bathroom and pressed them to her side, dismayed at how quickly they turned red.

Her eyes flickered.

My heart stuttered in my throat. "Marguerite?"

"Sandy?" she murmured.

"I'm right here."

Her head rolled from side to side. "It hurts."

"I know. I'm sorry."

"Not your fault," she mumbled, no strength in her words.

"I don't know how to help you."

"You need another file."

"I can't leave you here alone. Not like this."

She held my hand, her grip weak. "It's the only thing that will save me. Dreamland isn't fixed yet. Just one more…" Her eyes slid shut.

I stood and stared down at my Marguerite. *The Cat* curled up by her side. I couldn't leave her. But if I didn't, she would surely die. There was only one thing to do.

Buttoning my coat, I rushed out of the room, down three flights of stairs to the library. The shelves were filling as I entered. They were bursting with files. But there was space for more. We should have checked the shelves before. We should have realized. We'd celebrated too early.

Some of the files glowed. I didn't know what that meant. This was Marguerite's domain, but I plucked one at random, not bothering to read the details.

Moments later, I was back on Earth. If this didn't work, if I couldn't save Marguerite, there would be hell to pay.

Chapter Fourteen

SANDMAN

I ARRIVED in the middle of a large house, everything white and sterile, like the person who lived there didn't spend any time there. A wilting mixed bouquet made a centerpiece on a hall table and large windows revealed a view of the ocean. The scent of vanilla drifted in the air, and I noted the candle on a kitchen breakfast bar. I could see many rooms from my viewpoint.

I held the file open in my hands. I was just about to walk deeper into the house, to find a place to sit to read the file, when I noted the blinking light of an alarm. There were cameras everywhere. If I moved, I would set the alarm off.

Gritting my teeth, I resigned myself to staying put until the owner of the house returned. Glancing at the file, I noted her name was Maddison Powers. Her desire was to be satisfied by someone. Anyone. Male, female, a group, she didn't care. No one had ever been able to satisfy her or grant her an orgasm. She couldn't even pleasure herself. She'd get so far, and then...nothing.

I knew immediately who would be capable of fulfilling her dreams.

It took two hours for Maddison to return home. By that time it was dark and Marguerite had probably bled out. That probably wasn't true. Time passed differently in Dreamland, but I couldn't stop picturing her crumpled and broken body. I didn't want a new assistant. No one had ever died on me before.

The clink of keys sounded and then the door swung open. Maddison jabbed the code into the alarm. With dark shoulder length hair and wearing a tailored black suit to fit her figure, she presented an imposing air. She'd made her money in business. Sex toys specifically. But still could find none to satisfy herself.

She turned to face me. "I have a gun."

"I'm not here to hurt you," I said.

"You're standing in the middle of my house without an invitation. How did you get in here?"

"Sand."

"What?"

"Never mind."

"Who are you?"

"Most people call me The Sandman. Others call me Dream. Marguerite calls me Sandy. The gods call me the Keeper of Dreams."

"Who the hell is Marguerite? Wait...what? What do you want?"

"I want to grant you your wildest fantasies."

She clutched her stomach and laughed. "I don't want anything wild."

I tapped the file. "I know. You only want to be satisfied. A simple request."

She dropped her keys, then her handbag. Color leached from her face. "How do you know that?"

I tapped the file again.

"Are you from the press? If they knew the owner of Pleasure Ltd couldn't find satisfaction with any of her own toys..." she dared a step closer. "You don't look like a journalist."

"I'm not."

"Explain."

"Will you allow me to grant you your desire?"

A smile softened the tension in her angular face. "You're welcome to try."

Chapter Fifteen
MADDISON POWERS

SHAKING off the strange experience with the mysterious intruder, Maddison kicked off her heels and padded upstairs. The stranger had left, The Sandman, or whatever he called himself. Laughable really. And he really had blown sand at her. Ridiculous. Even weirder was that she did feel oddly tired. But her paperwork waited. Satisfaction reports on the new toys. If only.

With a glass of red wine in hand, Maddison sat on her bed and pulled the file that would keep her awake until the early hours of the morning onto her lap. She opened the folder, flicked through a few pages, took a couple sips of wine and allowed it to slip down her throat. It soothed her after a day on the phone, barking orders at staff. But at least the company was having its most profitable year.

She rubbed her feet together, longing to take a walk along the beach and dip her toes into the ocean. Maybe talk with that new neighbor who lived a few houses down. The handsome man with the rugged look about him. Maybe he could satisfy her.

Nope.

Not a chance. Maddison couldn't count the number of men she'd been with. And not because she had loose morals, but sex was sex, and females could enjoy a one-night stand just as much as a male, especially when they were only looking for one person. Just one. Just one person who could satisfy her. At forty-two years old, she still hadn't found him. Or her.

Sighing, Maddison tried to refocus on the papers in her lap, but her thoughts kept getting in her way. She closed the file, leaned back against the satin pillows, and sipped at her wine. Staring out her window, she watched a gray cat jump from a tree and onto her windowsill. It sat there in the open window, staring at her, its tail twitching, purring at her as if it had always lived there. A minute later, a second gray cat joined the first. Maddison frowned. She had nothing against animals. Would love to keep a pet, but her long hours wouldn't be fair on it. Equally, she didn't want to be the old spinster cat lady, either.

She was just about to get up and shoo them away when a woman appeared in her bedroom doorway. She was tall, even without heels, wearing some kind of flowing white dress that Maddison didn't realize was in fashion, but somehow fitted her perfectly. The dress was cinched with a gold belt at her waist that seemed to glow.

The woman fixed honey gold eyes on her, eyes Maddison couldn't look away from. She opened her mouth to speak, but no words came out. She could only take in the beauty of this strange woman standing in her bedroom.

"Please don't be alarmed," the woman said, drifting closer. "I've only come to help."

Maddison swung her feet to the floor. "Who are you?"

"I'm Freyja," the woman replied, as if that was all the explanation needed.

"You're the second person who has entered my house tonight without an invitation."

Freyja peered at her. "Do you need more sand?"

"Sand?" Maddison got to her feet. "What are you talking about?"

"Dream said you'd be pliable."

"Pliable!"

"That sounds worse than it is."

"Do you want to tell me what you're doing here before I call the cops?"

"I came to help grant you your desires."

Maddison laughed. "Not this again."

Freyja smiled, a smile filled with mischief and carnal knowledge.

"I don't need any help," Maddison said, glancing around the room for something she could use as a weapon.

"Sex is one of my specialties." Freyja walked across the room to the window. Both cats jumped into her arms and she nestled them close to her chest.

"Sex isn't the problem," Maddison snapped.

"My friends will help with the other bits."

"Other bits?" Maddison gaped at her.

"And I'm so glad you found my cats. I didn't know where they'd gotten to."

"They're yours?"

"Oh, yes. They drive my chariot."

"What the fuck is going on?" Maddison yelled.

Freyja looked up, giving no sign she'd been startled. "I'm Freyja, the Norse God of sex, among other things. And I'm here to help you achieve your desires."

Maddison would have laughed if they hadn't been interrupted by four men marching into the bedroom. She whirled around to face them, and couldn't escape the fact that most of them were half naked. And they were all beautiful. Perfect. Handsome. Striking. Even the one who was completely naked and sporting an enormous erection. Maddison had never seen anything so big. She wondered if he'd be up for making a cast for a new vibrator.

One man stepped forward. Dark hair. Dark eyes. A pair of small black wings sprouting from his shoulder blades. He carried a bow and quiver, which he rested on a chair as he approached. "I'm Cupid."

"*Cupid?*" Maddison gaped at him, aware her mouth was hanging open.

He wore only a loose pair of white trousers. His chest was bronzed and athletic, as if he shot arrows all day, every day. What would those muscular arms feel like around her?

"The one and only," Cupid replied with a cheeky grin. He seemed the youngest of them, and the most clean shaven.

Another man slapped Cupid's chest as he walked by. "I'm Eros. God of love." He was taller than Cupid. His hair darker and longer. His face broader and more masculine. His chest a solid wall of muscle. He stared at her, his eyes lit with desire.

Maddison cast a glance at the other two. The third male had dark brown skin and a pair of enormous white wings that floated above his head. His muscles were less obvious than the others, but his strength was apparent in his corded arms. He introduced himself as Himeros, God of sexual desire.

The fourth man, the one with the enormous erection that didn't seem capable of deflating, called himself Priapus, God of sexual intercourse. His skin was a luxurious brown, even all over his body as though he spent his days worshipping the sun...naked.

Maddison turned to Freyja, so many questions racing through her mind. "They think they can satisfy me? Give me an orgasm?"

Freyja nodded.

Maddison turned back to the men. "It doesn't matter how many you are, it will never happen."

Eros stepped forward, his eyes glinting. "But you have never been bedded by a god before, let alone five of us."

Freyja drew close to her, took her arm. "Will you at least allow us to try?"

Maddison glanced at the abandoned file on her bed. Work was the last thing she felt like doing. A stirring tingled between her legs. If this didn't work, then she would give up. But there was no harm in giving it one last try.

"Okay," Maddison said. "Let's do this."

A rush of activity made her dizzy as the men all promptly disrobed, revealing four throbbing erections of varying sizes, but all of them large enough to satisfy the hungriest of appetites. A pulsing ache built between her legs. A familiar one. She'd been here before.

Freyja removed a cloak and wrapped it around Maddison's shoulders.

"What's this for?" Maddison asked, as Freyja's hands moved over the buttons of her shirt.

"Let's just say it will keep you interested," the blonde goddess replied as she finished undoing Maddison's buttons. She pulled the shirt from Maddison, then slid off her skirt until she was standing only in her bra, panties, and stockings. Within seconds, those were off too, but Freyja wrapped the cloak around her and concealed her modesty. "Please, sit on the bed and enjoy your wine."

Feeling a little like a princess from long ago, Maddison made her way to her bed, and crawled onto the satin sheets. Propping herself against the pillows, she arranged the cloak around herself, aware of her nakedness beneath, and sipped on her wine.

Eros crawled onto the bed and sat to her right. He lounged on an elbow, his erection pushing into her thigh. Cupid draped himself by her left, his small wings fluttering and tickling her cheek. While Himeros, the god with the enormous white wings, found an armchair to sit in. He crossed his legs, but it didn't hide anything.

That left a naked Priapus standing in the middle of the room. After shooing her cats away, Freyja approached him. They faced each other in the middle of the room. Maddison's breath quickened as Priapus reached around Freyja's back and undid her dress. The sheer fabric slipped off her shoulders and pooled on the thick carpet.

She was completely naked underneath. Maddison admired the fullness of the goddess' breasts, the shape of her slender hips, the curve of her stomach. She'd never taken the time to examine the female form before. Yes, she'd had nights with women in the past, but few had existed beyond a drunken lay that never got her off.

"You're so beautiful," Maddison murmured.

Eros edged closer to her, his erection pressing harder into her thigh. Cupid slipped a hand under the cloak and rested it on her hip. Maddison bit back a sharp inhale at the touch. Nothing had ever excited her so much. That one touch, the warmth of his hand resting on her body, sent a pressure throbbing through her moistening folds and deep into her center. She wanted this. Oh God, she wanted this.

Freyja cupped her breasts and offered them to Priapus. He rubbed a thumb over a nipple, cradled the other, then brought his mouth to Freyja's breasts. He kissed and licked and nipped until Maddison could almost feel it herself.

"I love some tits!" Himeros called from the chair, his eyes smoldering, his hand around his erect penis.

Cupid's hand moved from Maddison's hip, traveled the small distance to her waist, then back to her hip. Back and forth, a delicate touch, caressing her. Maddison let out an involuntary moan. *God, please, God, make it happen.*

Priapus sat back in a chair with no armrests, side on, so Maddison could watch the profile of his straining shaft. Freyja hovered over him, her eyes on his erection. She spread her legs and straddled him. Standing, she hovered over her fellow god.

Maddison bit her lip to prevent herself from calling out. Cupid's hand drifted below her hip, edging toward the small patch of hair hiding her need. A twinge of pleasure pulsed through her.

On her other side, Eros slid his hand into the cloak and took one of her breasts in his hands. Ever so gently, he rubbed his thumb over her nipple, gently coaxing. Maddison's limbs went to jelly. Pleasure pulsed deep inside. Wetness gathered and the smell of it filled the air.

Freyja lowered herself onto Priapus' shaft, taking him in inch by inch, ever so slowly, so Maddison could watch every moment. When Priapus disappeared inside her, he let out a sigh and threw his head back. "That is the best feeling in the world. You're always so fucking tight, Freyja. I could fuck you every day, all day. And then every night too."

"It's my pleasure," Freyja replied as she started to grind against him.

"Oh. My. God," Maddison murmured. Her toes twitched with anticipation. The moist warmth between her lips begged to be satisfied.

"You called?" Eros winked.

Maddison laughed. "You really are all gods."

Cupid's hand moved to her clit, just brushing the tip. Maddison let out a groan, her body shuddering at the spike of sensation. Eros parted the cloak, revealing both her breasts. Both his hands caressed her, teasing her nipples. He lowered his head and sucked on them, drawing them into his warm mouth. She'd never felt anything so good.

Freyja's quickening breath made her snap her eyes

open to watch once more. The blonde goddess bucked and grinded against Priapus. He clutched at her buttocks, drawing her closer, pushing himself in deeper.

"That's it baby, you're going to come now, aren't you?" Freyja teased.

"I am going to come in you and fill you up to your fucking eyeballs, then I'm going to turn you over and do it to you all over again," Priapus yelled.

"Can't wait," Freyja replied, digging her hands into his shoulders.

They came at the same time, Priapus' shouts low and guttural, Freyja's screams bringing the house down.

"Yes, yes, yes, yes," Freyja repeated as the orgasm pounded through her.

Maddison could only watch, completely transfixed.

When it was over, Freyja climbed off Priapus and approached the bed. She kneeled on the floor at the bottom of the bed and took one of Maddison's toes into her mouth. Himeros finally moved from his chair, his hand on his cock, stroking up and down. He crawled onto the bed and pressed his pulsating penis next to Maddison's cheek. She turned her head, searching for the engorged shaft with her tongue. Licking the head, her tongue worked hard, causing the god to groan and slit his eyes closed.

"That's right, you're so good at that, aren't you?" Himeros murmured.

Cupid moved his hand to her clitoris. He caressed her with a single finger, pushing and stroking until her need almost exploded. Her mouth worked harder on Himeros while Cupid's pace increased, causing sensations to gather in her depths. The pleasure hovered, threatening to come, but she knew it wouldn't. It never had before, no matter what they did.

Eros touched her breasts, grasped them roughly in his large hands, murmured dirty thoughts in her ear.

"You know you want to."

"It will be the best orgasm you've ever had."

"You're going to come like a bitch and beg us to visit you every night."

"That sweet, wet cunt is all any of us want."

She couldn't reply. She was full of Himeros in her mouth. He bucked deeper into her, reaching her throat. But she took him all, loving the taste of him, marveling at the idea of giving a god pleasure.

Fingers moved inside her wetness. She gasped, almost biting Himeros' penis. But he only groaned louder as her mouth tightened around him.

Cupid worked his fingers inside her, moving harder and faster and finding her g-spot. She bucked as the pleasure tormented her. She was close. *So damn close.* She'd never wanted anything more.

Eros took a turn. He dribbled wine from her glass on her stomach, lapped it up with his tongue. Then he dripped it onto the point of her clit, poured it inside her. He placed his mouth over her folds, sucking the wine back out, groaning all the time. Her mind almost exploded with the dizzying sensations. His mouth drew in her pulsing point. Nipping, biting, licking. And then his tongue was inside her. Himeros continued to thrust into her mouth. Pleasure swarmed over her flesh. She didn't know what to feel, where to feel it, but she didn't want any of it to stop.

Something shifted deep inside her center. A release of pressure. Small, but unmistakable. Maddison let out a groan. Himeros withdrew for a moment, and the groan became a scream. She bucked and writhed on the bed, reaching for Eros' head to push his tongue deeper. But he moved away.

"Please. *Please*," she begged. "It was happening."

Suddenly Eros was on top of her, lowering himself, pushing himself into her. His deep penetration sent a spasm shuddering through her body. She bit onto his shoulder to prevent herself releasing the welling scream.

"That's it, you can do it," Cupid murmured in her ear.

Himeros reentered her mouth. Freyja was doing something nice to her toes. Priapus hovered at the end of the bed, his eternal erection proud and enormous, watching the whole thing with a gleam in his eyes.

She took her mouth off Himeros, placed her hand around his shaft and stroked with fast movements. She did the same to Cupid on her other side. One dick inside her, one in each hand. Eros shifted her so she was sitting on top of him. He thrust into her with powerful strokes, tantalizing her insides, hammering a series of spasms through her.

A pressure at her anus. Priapus stood behind her, pressing himself into her asshole. She'd never done that before. Couldn't think of anything else she wanted more in that moment.

"Yes," she said to him over her shoulder.

As Eros thrust into her, she gyrated against him.

Priapus pushed himself into her other entrance. And still her hands worked around Cupid and Himeros.

Priapus was inside her. Eros was inside her. Together, they worked a rhythm that almost sent her over the edge. She could barely move, could only circle her hips. Each of their thrusts sent new spasms pounding through her.

She'd never been this close before. The orgasm tantalized her. Her clitoris felt like it was on fire. Within her swollen depths, the pleasure throbbed. She took both Eros and Priapus as deep as she could. The sensations mounted, pounded through her core, her clit, her entire body. A wave of abandon crashed over her. She gripped the two shafts of Cupid and Himeros as she threw her head back and roared. A roar of release. A roar of pure ecstasy. A roar of fulfilment.

The orgasm throbbed through her, taking no prisoners, shuddering through every muscle and nerve ending in her body. The depths of her soaking center vibrated with bliss. Her clitoris pulsed with the sweetness of release. And still she screamed.

Cupid and Himeros ejaculated at the same time, their cum covering her chest, making her movements slick against Eros. Neither of them cared. Both Eros and Priapus continued to thrust into her. Never had she felt so full, so fulfilled.

Letting go of Cupid and Himeros, she gripped onto Eros' shoulders. Freyja was there, capturing her lips, kissing her so hard she couldn't breathe.

Eros and Priapus worked together. They didn't let up. One orgasm wasn't enough. A second hammered through her. Deeper and more intense than the first. As she yelled out her pleasure, both Priapus and Eros thrust deep, kept themselves inside, not moving, allowing the spasms to tear her apart.

She bucked against them, circling her hips, working both of them at the same time. Eros came first. Deep inside her, his warmth adding to her abating pleasure. Then Priapus in her back entrance.

They kept her propped up between them, both of their penises throbbing. It was enough to drive another orgasm into her. The third one tingled deep in her soaked vagina, spreading out through her thighs, her limbs, tingled at the back of her neck, consumed her entire body. It ripped through her sodden depths, ebbed into her swollen folds, spilled into the tip of her quivering clitoris. It didn't give up. She could barely contain the sensation. She screamed loud and long as her muscles contracted and the orgasm poured out of her.

Spent, she collapsed back onto the bed as Eros and Priapus pulled themselves out of her. Freyja came at her with a bowl of warm water and a towel, dabbing her naked body, cleaning her up.

The men curled around her on the bed, their eyes roaming her body, their expressions contented.

"Thank you," Maddison said. "Thank you so fucking much."

"No one has been able to take all five of us at once before." Freyja wiped the warm towel over her body.

"That was impressive," Cupid said.

"We're not done yet," Eros said.

"There's plenty more where that came from," Priapus said, the only one still sporting an erection.

Himeros' wings floated above their heads. "I want a taste of that delicious cunt."

Cupid nudged him. "You can get in line, I'm next."

Madison giggled, reached for them all, whispered sweet sentiments to them. They had the whole night ahead of them. One entire blissful night. They could demand anything of her and she would give it to them.

An idea for a new line of sex toys came into her mind. Something based on the gods. New vibrators. New toys. Names like ecstasy, bliss, pleasure, and more. Or maybe she'd name them after the gods themselves.

For now, Maddison was exhausted. She took a sip of wine and allowed her eyes to slide closed. Just a little nap. Then back to the gods in her bed.

Chapter Sixteen

SANDMAN

Back in Dreamland, I ran through the halls, up two flights of stairs, and threw open the door to my bedroom. The sheets were a tangled mess. There were bloody towels on the floor, but no Marguerite. *The Cat* stalked miserably across the carpet.

"Where is she?"

It only mewed plaintively in response.

I retraced my steps, dashing through the halls, screaming her name, listening out for anything more than an echo.

Did she die? In my absence, had she died? Had I not done enough to keep her alive? And now I would be here alone. They wouldn't grant me a new assistant after a fuck up like this. Not that I would want one.

I hovered at the top of the steps that led to the library, a hand in my pocket, feeling the reassuring grains of sand. If she wasn't here...

With no further delays, I charged down the staircase and dashed through the grand arched entrance to the library. Turning in a wild circle, I searched for Marguerite among the crowded shelves and glowing folders. A hint of red, there.

"Marguerite!" I called, running after the flash of red hair.

She stuck her head around an aisle. Smiled. "Sandy! You're back."

"You're the only one who calls me that," I said, although there were a million other sentiments I wanted to express.

"I know."

"You're okay?"

She nodded, smoothed down her clothes. "Perfectly."

"But you were hurt...all that blood..." I approached her, inspecting her for signs of injury.

"You saved me by granting more dreams." She performed a slow spin, held her hands wide. "As good as new."

"Thank God." I eased myself into a chair.

Marguerite approached and sat on the edge of the desk. "God had nothing to do with it. It was all you."

I waved a hand. "You think too much of me."

"And you think too little."

I sighed and propped my chin on my hand. "Dreamland? Have we done enough?"

She indicated the crammed and glowing shelves. "Back to normal. You should see outside."

"No thank you," I replied. "The last outing was adventurous enough for me."

She sighed, crossed her arms.

I was immediately alert. "What is it?"

"I'm disappointed."

Was she finally going to tell me what she wanted? Not needed, but wanted.

"What's the matter?" My heart paused in my chest. It had never done that before.

"You've been here for centuries."

"We both have," I said.

"And yet you've learned nothing."

I frowned, casting my mind back to our more recent conversations, searching for the moment when I'd missed something.

Marguerite reached a hand into my pocket and brought out a pinch of sand. "It's time for you to learn what your true desires are."

Before I could protest, she blew the sand at me and I fell asleep in my chair.

Chapter Seventeen

SANDMAN

VOICES FILLED THE PALACE. Voices that had never been in Dreamland before. Voices that shouldn't be here now.

I left the sand cellar where I'd been grinding angels' tears, and dashed up the stairs, following the foreign noises. My boots echoed on the tiles, a discordant sound I'd never noticed before. But now I was trying to be discreet.

There was nothing menacing about the voices; they were light and airy and without a trace of threat, but still, there shouldn't be anyone here. Unless the gods had returned to punish me for putting Marguerite in danger. But their voices would sound dark and foreboding.

I rounded the corner into the great hall to find five familiar faces gathered in a loose clump. Rose Tanner; dreamer of shifters and wolves. Samantha Morrison; dreamer of a long-lost love. Lucius DeVille; dreamer of the perfect relationship. Bethany James; dreamer of sexual awakening. Maddison Powers; dreamer of fulfillment.

I frowned. "What are you all doing here?"

"We came to visit you," Maddison said, a fresh glow giving warmth to her angular features.

"But mortals aren't allowed in Dreamland."

Lucius stepped forward, ever the negotiator. "This is *your* dream, Dream Keeper. Anything can happen."

"But why would I dream all of you?"

Bethany approached, fingered the lapels of my black coat, tugged on them in a way I wasn't sure I liked. "I think we could all teach you a thing or two about desire."

"Desire?" I gulped as I cast a quick glance at the stairs. What would Marguerite do if she found them here? "I think I need to wake up."

"It's not so fun, is it, when the shoe is on the other foot, so to speak?" Maddison said, a hint of laughter playing through her smile. "Strangers barging into your house."

"I'm sorry. I only wanted to help."

"You did," Samantha said. Gone were the baggy plaid shirt and milk stains. She wore black skinny jeans with a cashmere sweater and a delicate silver chain at her neck. Simple. Elegant. Beautiful. "You helped all of us."

"And now we want to show you the same gratitude," Rose said.

I raised both palms. "Really, you don't owe me anything. It's my job."

"There's that word again," Lucius said. "Life is more than work."

"Is there somewhere more private we can go?" Maddison asked, causing Bethany to giggle. "I'd hate to be interrupted."

"Interrupted?" I didn't like the screech in my voice.

"Come on." Maddison grabbed my sleeve and tugged me along after her. "This fancy palace is bound to have a parlor or something."

Mute, I could only follow as I wondered how I could cast them out of Dreamland. If it was one of their dreams, they wouldn't be able to interact with me. Which meant it had to be my dream. I'd never dreamed before. I'd never given myself the luxury.

"A-ha!" Rose clapped when Maddison threw open a door. It was the sitting room. One of the smaller receiving rooms that hadn't been used in years, crammed full of overstuffed furniture. Comfortable sofas and deep armchairs. Heavy drapes framed the windows. A few books lay scattered around, along with a few of my lightning sculptures. "This is perfect."

"Sit." Maddison pushed me onto a couch with one finger.

"Relax, take a load off," Bethany said as she helped me out of my coat.

Lucius sat opposite me, a carnal grin propped on his lips. "This is going to be such fun."

"What is?" I asked, finding my voice.

"Finding out what you desire, silly," Rose said as she sat next to me. Her fingers stepped a line along my thigh, getting dangerously close to areas I wasn't sure I wanted her near.

"You are seriously uptight," Bethany said as she sat on the other side of me. "For someone whose job it is to grant dreams, you'd think you'd be a little more chilled."

"I take my job very seriously," I replied, cursing the indignation in my tone.

Maddison stood behind me. She bent over, her breath whisking close to my cheek. She reached down and undid a button on my shirt.

"Hey!" I protested.

"Do you want to find out what your true desire is?" Maddison hissed in my ear.

"I know what my desires are."

"What? Tell us then?" Rose asked.

I looked at them all, their earnest expressions, but couldn't bring the right words to mind. I slouched into the couch. "It's private. Dreamland has changed. And Marguerite has been ever so—"

The women giggled at the sound of her name.

"Ever so...?" Lucius whisked a hand and urged me to continue.

"Helpful," I finished.

"Is that all?" Maddison asked as she trailed a painted fingernail under my shirt.

"She's been instrumental in running Dreamland," I added, watching Rose's hand creep up my thigh.

"Let us help you find the answer," Lucius said. He held a glass of whisky in his hand. I had no idea where he'd gotten it. But then dreams were like that.

Maddison undid the buttons on my shirt. Rose helped me slip out of it. Bethany eyed up my trousers.

"Relax," Bethany said. "If I can do it, so can you."

"It's not my first time," I muttered.

Maddison undid my belt, then my trousers. There

was no hiding my arousal as her hands brushed against me. My trousers came off. Things were happening quickly. I didn't know if they were the right things.

I sat on the couch in only my black boxer shorts. Rose nibbled on my ear. Maddison's hands roamed my chest. Bethany tucked her hand between my legs, into my boxer shorts, her hand circling my erection. *God, that felt good.*

I found myself flat on my back, all three of the women touching and kissing. Lucius knew I didn't want him in that way, so seemed content to watch and offer suggestions.

Bethany began stroking my shaft gently, testing, but I could barely endure the sensations. Rose's hands raked through my hair. But it was Maddison who straddled my waist and kissed me. Her lips pressed down on me, her tongue parting mine, searching inside my mouth.

My erection throbbed. It pulsed with longing, and a deep ache settled in my loins. How easy it would be to give in to it all. Bethany's hand moved faster, up and down my shaft, coaxing a groan out of my mouth. Maddison's mouth on my chest, Rose's at my throat.

A flash of red in my mind. A smile like no other. Creamy skin that blew my mind. A kindness that stole my heart.

I lurched upright, throwing the women off me. "This isn't what I want."

"Have you discovered your true desire?" Lucius asked, his fingers steepled over a knee.

I stood, panted for air. "Yes." *How can I have been so stupid?*

I stood there in my boxer shorts, in the flowery parlor, shivering with indecision.

"Go!" Bethany flicked a hand at me. "Go get your true desire."

I left them, left the parlor that I hadn't used in years, and ran through the halls. Somehow, by the time I reached the library, I was fully clothed again.

Marguerite turned at my approach, the small movement filling the large room with her tantalizing scent. One I couldn't begin to describe. "You're back."

"I'm am." I laid a hand over my chest, willing my heart to slow down.

"Did you dream?" Moonlight played across her eyelashes, picking out flecks of gold.

"I did," I said, leaning on a desk to catch my breath.

"How was it?"

"Enlightening."

She tilted her head. "I feel like there's more."

I smiled at her. "So much more."

"Shall I put on a pot of tea?"

"No," I said, closing the distance between us. "No. There's no time for tea."

"No time?" She put the file she'd been holding on a table, pressed her fingertips into the solid wood. Her hair tumbled over her shoulder. Hair I desperately wanted to touch, to wrap around my hands, to bury my face in. Hair I wanted to move away from her cheek so I could kiss the flawless skin of her neck, her throat, her jaw...her everything.

"I've been so foolish."

"Have you now?" She leaned into me.

"I know what you want."

"You do? What about what *you* want?" She searched my face for answers.

I didn't shy away from her penetrating stare. "I know that too."

"You do?" she asked, her fingers lightly brushing mine.

"We want the same," I said, and took her in my arms.

She pressed herself against me as I lowered my lips to hers. In all the years we'd spent together, how had I not seen it before? Marguerite had always been my favorite. But I hadn't allowed myself to feel. I hadn't dared hope that I was permitted to have such emotions. But I couldn't deny them any longer.

Her scent overwhelmed me, made my knees buckle. To steady myself, I circled my arms around her waist, breathed her in until my throat ached with her scent. The feel of her hair falling over my face was enough to drive me over the edge. The touch of her warm breath on my skin drove the love deep into my heart. The curve of her breast pressed against my chest, a promise of more. A promise of everything.

We had touched countless times before, but not like this. This was entirely new. A heady experience that caused my breath to hitch.

"Do you feel it too?" she whispered.

"I feel everything," I said as the weight of love almost crushed me.

I kissed her softly, learning the feel of her lips, exploring her taste. And then the years of pent-up passion took over. I moved my hand to the back of her neck, cradled her closer, allowing the kiss to turn heated and heavy.

"Oh, Sandy," Marguerite murmured between kisses, her hands curling into my coat.

I moved my lips to her perfect ear. "I love you."

She pulled away. "Do you truly mean that?"

I laid a hand over my heart. "With every ounce of my being."

She claimed my lips this time, her teasing tongue darting between them. I drowned in her touch, gave into the smell of her, the feel of her. Nothing had ever made me feel so complete. She drew my tongue into her mouth, possessing it hungrily. I covered her wanton groans with my mouth.

Pulling back, she took my hand in hers as a mischievous grin took over her lips. "Let's go upstairs."

Without a word, she led me out of the library, up the stairs. We bypassed the hall leading to the bedrooms and instead found our way to our favorite balustrade. There, she kissed me again and pulled me tight against her. Her breasts pressed against my chest. How I wanted to touch those perfect mounds of alluring flesh, to bury my face in them, to take them in my mouth. But we were exposed on the balcony, for all of Dreamland to watch.

"People will see," I said.

"There's no one else here."

Of course not.

I held her face in my hands, kissing her and kissing her and kissing her, until that wasn't enough.

I buried my face in her neck, laying soft kisses on her

smooth skin, following the line of her collarbone as I'd seen so many mortals do in their dreams. Reaching for the buttons on her dress, I hesitated. There would be no coming back from this. This simple mortal act would undo me, bind me to her for all eternity.

"I love you, Sandy."

I cast any remaining doubts aside.

She helped me out of my coat. I no longer cared about the spilled sand. She threaded her arms out of her dress and finally I could kiss her again. Her throat, her chest, the pleasing swell of her breasts. I teased the tight bud of her nipple with my tongue, then drew it into my mouth, tasting it, toying with it, until she clutched me tight and groaned in my ear.

Then her hands were on me, undoing the buttons on my shirt, which quickly became a disregarded pile on the floor. Her hands brushed over my chest, my back, my arms, touching me everywhere, learning me as if she were blind.

We leaned against the balustrade, neither of us feeling the cold of the stone. My arousal strained against my trousers, and I could no longer bear to be separated from her, even if it was by the merest amount of fabric. We would only be whole once we were connected. Physically. Emotionally. For all eternity.

Marguerite must have sensed my need, for she released my erection, pushing my trousers and boxer shorts off, until I stood naked in the moonlight cradling the woman of my dreams.

I left a trail of kisses down her taut stomach, over the

curve of her hips, against the damp point of her pleasure. She gasped, her hands delving through my hair once more, gripping at the roots.

"I want you up here, Sandy," she whispered, pulling me to my feet.

She shifted onto the balustrade, spread her legs, waiting for me. Her sweet smell surrounded us, making me crave more of her. All of her.

I savored the moment, taking in her exquisitely naked form. Her translucent skin glowed in the moonlight and her red hair trailed a breath of fire down her back. Her pale blue eyes glinted with desire, and I realized it had always been there. It was me who'd been so blind.

Marguerite took my hand. "What are you thinking, Sandy?"

"How beautiful you are."

I studied her face, the point of her delicate nose, the shape of her inviting smile, the curve of her rosy cheek, and my heart thudded painfully between my ribs. I'd never wanted anything more.

She stared back at me, bit down on her lip, which caused my erection to throb. I wanted her so much, but I wanted to savor every second of this experience.

My gaze dropped to the length of her elegant neck, my fingers following the path of my eyes, leaving a gentle touch. She shivered and moved my hand to her breast. I molded the swollen mound gently in my hand as I dropped my gaze even lower. Down the length of her taut stomach and to the thatch of downy red curls hiding her need.

Marguerite kissed my knuckles. "I want you, Sandy."

"And I want you."

Her fingertips skated across my aching erection, then gripped more firmly around my shaft. A shudder of pleasure pulsed through me and my eyes slitted.

"Come closer," she whispered, pulling me by my throbbing hardness.

She guided me toward her entrance. I felt the warmth of her surround the head of my penis. Gripping her arms, I held her close to me. As she guided me inside, I kissed her, taking her small moans into my mouth.

"Push," she said as she released her hand.

I pushed myself into her silken center, gliding smoothly until I filled her depths.

"Oh, Sandy," she murmured in my ear, then followed it with a series of gentle kisses and nibbles on my lobe.

I wrapped my hands around her, gripped her buttocks, holding her in place on the balustrade. I began with slow and gentle strokes, almost slipping entirely out of her each time. And each time I plunged into her, she'd let out a groan of pleasure. It drove me crazy; her satisfied sighs at my ear.

I held her against me, one hand cradling the back of her neck, the other gripping her buttocks tight. Her breasts pressed tightly against my chest. My mouth on her neck. I thrust into her again and again. Never had anything elicited such pleasure. Such bliss. No wonder mortals dreamed of sexual desire so often.

"Harder," she whispered.

I pushed harder, deeper, keeping my strokes even. My

shaft swelled with the anticipation of release, yet still I kept thrusting into her.

Her hips moved against me. She clutched the back of my neck, anchoring herself as her body bucked and writhed.

Suddenly, she threw her head back, her body jerking against me, and screamed into the night. The angels in the sky played their harps, smiling down at us, and the unicorns charged through the meadows.

The pressure built at the base of my shaft, thundered its way to the tip, and then finally a release so powerful I could only groan into Marguerite's hair. My entire body shuddered as the waves of pleasure moved through me, pulsing through my hardness, throbbing into her silken depths.

"That's it, Sandy. That's it," Marguerite whispered in my ear as my seed filled her wet center.

"Oh my God," I muttered as I collapsed against her.

We stood there together, still connected, as I let my head drop to her shoulder. "Thank you. Thank you for—"

"Shhh." Marguerite hushed me with a kiss. "We've got all of eternity to talk. To make love."

That was true.

The Cat looked at us curiously. We both burst out laughing, scaring it away.

I pulled out of her, still hard with desire, and carried her to my bedroom. I needed more. And during that first night together, she showed me many of the ways mortals dreamed. Things I'd never heard of. Feelings I'd never felt. Sensations that almost broke me. I loved each and everything she did to me. Everything I did to her.

Marguerite and I added our dreams to Dreamland. It never fell into disrepair again.

The End

If you enjoyed *Dream Keeper*, please consider leaving a review here:
https://geni.us/TheDreamKeeper

Thank You!

Thank you so much for making it all the way to the end.

I hope you have enjoyed *Dream Keeper* and are excited to start dreaming tonight! If you did, leaving a review is the best possible present for an author! You can do it here:

https://geni.us/TheDreamKeeper

Fantasy lands and characters have always fascinated me, and the character of The Sandman has been with me for years. I loved the idea of a sexy sandman and enjoyed discovering his inner most desires as I wrote this book.

About the Author

Savannah Wilde is the pen name for a best-selling, award winning young adult and new adult author. After joining booktok, she quickly discovered a penchant for smut, and realized that publishers wouldn't want an overly spicy YA novel, so delved into the realm of steamy fantasy romance with a new pen name and hasn't looked back. This is her first spicy novel.

Savannah loves to hear from her readers. You can connect with her at the links below.

Twitter: @SpicyAuthor
Instagram: @SpicyAuthorSavannah
Tiktok: @ SpicyAuthorSavannah